Aberdeenshire Library and Information Service
www.aberdeenshire.gov.uk/libraries
Renewals Hotline 01224 661511

Shelby watched, along with everyone else, as the expensive-looking loafer touched the pavement. In one athletic movement a man slipped out of the low car. His gaze met hers through the window. Her breath caught in her throat. His piercing look made her wonder if he could see secrets she'd kept hidden. He gave her a slight nod of acknowledgement.

His gaze traveled back and forth along the line of stores in the mostly abandoned strip mall. If it hadn't been for the brief twist of contempt marring his looks he would've qualified for the term "dangerously attractive."

How dared he act as if Benton was beneath him? After her husband, Jim, died continuing to live and work here had been the best decision she'd ever made. The community had supported her one hundred and ten percent as she grieved. Each person had their own little quirks but they all had big hearts.

The new doctor still held the room's attention as he stepped to the door and pulled. The front of his car rested so far over the sidewalk that it wouldn't allow the door to open far enough for him to enter.

Shelby couldn't stop the twitch of her lips as she checked a chuckle. He was making a notable first impression on the locals sitting in the waiting room. Everyone in town would be enjoying this story by bedtime.

Dear Reader

Sometimes people 'drive fast and live hard' in order to forget the past. They run away, hoping the further they get from their memories the less those memories will matter. Others use their job to replace an intimate relationship. Of course Shelby and Taylor are no different, so that's why I loved seeing them fight their feelings and find their happily-ever-after. I hope you appreciate Shelby's and Taylor's story as much as I enjoyed writing it. Theirs wasn't a smooth road to love, but I had a good time travelling along with them just the same.

I would be remiss if I didn't mention the issue of bullying, which happens so often to school-age children. It's important to call attention to this issue and stop it when we can. So many children and young adults live with horrible memories of their childhood because they were bullied. If you see it happening intervene, and share a positive word with the person being hurt. You might very well be the one person who makes a difference in that child's life.

Even though the places and people in this story are fictitious, the setting of west Tennessee holds a special place in my heart. I spent part of my childhood living there, and still enjoy returning every now and then. It's a beautiful part of the US, and the people are always warm and welcoming when I visit.

I love to hear from my readers. Stop by and say hi at www.SusanCarlisle.com. I promise to say hi back!

Happy reading!

Susan

HOT-SHOT DOC COMES TO TOWN

BY
SUSAN CARLISLE

To Mom. For all your love and support.

First published in Great Britain 2013
by Mills & Boon, an imprint of Harlequin (UK) Limited.
Large Print edition 2013
Harlequin (UK) Limited, Eton House,
18-24 Paradise Road, Richmond, Surrey TW9 1SR

© Susan Carlisle 2013

ISBN: 978 0 263 23120 5

Harlequin (UK) policy is to use papers that are natural, renewable and recyclable products and made from wood grown in sustainable forests. The logging and manufacturing process conform to the legal environmental regulations of the country of origin.

Printed and bound in Great Britain
by CPI Antony Rowe, Chippenham, Wiltshire

LP

Susan Carlisle's love affair with books began when she made a bad grade in math in the sixth grade. Not allowed to watch TV until she'd brought the grade up, she filled her time with books and became a voracious romance reader. She has 'keepers' on the shelf to prove it. Because she loved the genre so much she decided to try her hand at creating her own romantic worlds. She still loves a good happily-ever-after-story.

When not writing Susan doubles as a high school substitute teacher, which she has been doing for sixteen years. Susan lives in Georgia with her husband of twenty-eight years and has four grown children. She loves castles, travelling, cross-stitching, hats, James Bond and hearing from her readers.

Recent titles by the same author:

THE NURSE HE SHOULDN'T NOTICE
HEART SURGEON, HERO...HUSBAND?

**Also available in eBook format
from www.millsandboon.co.uk**

CHAPTER ONE

THE flash of red in the parking space directly in front of the Benton Clinic door caught Dr. Shelby Wayne's attention. Great, this could only be the bad-boy doctor her uncle had told her to expect, and over six hours late.

Squinting, she looked through the dusty plate-glass window at the slick convertible sports car on the other side. As far as she knew, no one in that area of western Tennessee had a car nearly as fine as the one now almost blocking the door. This was big-truck not fancy-car country.

Babysitting her Uncle Gene's most recent personal project wasn't her idea of a good time. But needing help at the clinic so badly meant she couldn't send him back to Nashville. Still if she could get two weeks' worth of free medical help out of it, she'd bend over backwards to accommodate her uncle. Maybe if she played her cards right she could convince the doctor that his skills would be better utilized in Benton than where he was currently working.

If she wanted the clinic to remain open, she'd have to find some help soon.

She glanced at the clipboard for the name of her next patient then scanned the packed waiting room for Mrs. Stewart. It would be a waste of time to try to get the attention of the sweet little grandmotherly woman with a hearing problem over the din in the tiny room. As she walked towards Mrs. Stewart the people waiting quieted, and all eyes turned to look out the window.

Shelby watched, along with everyone else, as the expensive-looking loafer touched the pavement. In one athletic movement a man slipped out of the low car. His gaze met hers through the window. Her breath caught in her throat. His piercing look made her wonder if he could see secrets she'd kept hidden. He gave her a slight nod of acknowledgement.

His gaze traveled back and forth along the line of stores in the mostly abandoned strip mall. If it hadn't been for the brief twist of contempt marring his looks he would've qualified for the term "dangerously attractive".

How dared he act as if Benton was beneath

him? After her husband Jim had died, continuing to live and work here had been the best decision she'd ever made. Her parents had encouraged her to move back to her home town to practice but she'd decided Benton was where she belonged. It was where she and Jim had chosen to make their home. Benton had supported her a hundred and ten percent as she'd grieved. Each person had their own little quirks but they all had a big hearts. Here she felt secure.

The new doctor still held the room's attention as he stepped to the door and pulled. The front of his car rested so far over the sidewalk that it wouldn't allow the door to open far enough for him to enter.

Shelby couldn't stop the twitch of her lips as she checked a chuckle. He was making a notable first impression on the locals sitting in the waiting room. Everyone in town would be enjoying this story by bedtime. That was one of the great things about living in a small town, though it could also be the worst. Everyone knew everything. When you had a tragedy your friends and neighbors were there to support you, but when there was a good story to tell they spread it.

The man snarled and murmured a sharp word

under his breath. Turning, he took three quick strides back to the driver's door, opened it and slid behind the wheel with the same grace as when he'd alighted. Leaving one leg hanging outside the open door, he started the car. The windows of the clinic vibrated slightly as he backed the vehicle up until the entire sidewalk could be seen. As quickly as he'd started the car he shut off the engine, got out and slammed the door.

His long strides brought him towards the entrance of the clinic again. The only indication in his demeanor that he might still be annoyed was the jerk he gave the clinic door.

Shelby smiled but not too broadly so that he wouldn't think she'd been laughing at him. "You must be Dr. Stiles. I was expecting you hours ago."

"Are you Dr. Wayne?"

She offered him her hand. "I'm Dr. Shelby Wayne."

He shook her hand. "With the name Shelby I had expected a man. Taylor Stiles."

His clasp was firm. Warm and dry. Not the dead-fish handshake she'd anticipated from the fancy-dressed, showy-car-driving, big-city doctor.

"Sorry to disappoint you," Shelby said with a hint of sarcasm.

"If you two young people are through putting on a show..." Mrs. Stewart looked pointedly at Taylor Stiles "...and making nice, would one of you mind seeing about my sciatica?"

Taylor blinked in surprise. As if on cue, the room erupted in noise as though the curtain had closed and the play was over.

Shelby cleared her throat. She loved the outspoken and to-the-point woman. "Uh, yes, Mrs. Stewart. You're next." Shelby handed the clipboard to Dr. Stiles. "Call the next patient under Mrs. Stewart's name and put him or her in room two." She pointed down the short hallway. "I'll be in after I see Mrs. Stewart."

Dr. Stiles's dashing brow rose a fraction of an inch but he accepted the clipboard. Apparently he wasn't used to taking direction. His deep baritone voice called little Greg Hankins's name while she guided Mrs. Stewart to exam room one.

"Kind of snooty, that one, but still mighty handsome," Mrs. Stewart remarked as she took a seat in the chair in the room.

"Um, I guess," Shelby said as she flipped through the seventy-four-year-old's chart.

"I could tell by the look on your face you noticed it too. Doc Shelby, you have to start living again. It's been three years. Your Jim is dead, not you."

A stab of pain came with that frank statement about her husband. There had been nothing she could do when she'd reached the accident. Despite not being far behind Jim in her own car, his truck had already been wrapped around a tree when she arrived at the scene. Nothing she'd done had stopped his blood from pooling in the mangled metal. The sight, the smell… She'd retched. Three years later she could at least do everything in her power to honor his memory by keeping the clinic open any way she could. The people of Benton she loved so much needed the medical care and she needed the security of knowing she was needed.

"Now, Mrs. Stewart…" Shelby smiled "…I'm supposed to be taking care of you, not you seeing about me."

"Well, missy, I think you don't want to see about you, so I'm just going to have to."

Shelby took a deep breath and let it out slowly. "Why don't you let me examine you, then we can work on me?" Adjusting her bright pink stethoscope in her ears, she placed the disk on the woman's chest.

"All you think about is this clinic. Maybe with Dr. Kildare here you can have a little fun for a change," the old woman groused.

"Dr. Kildare?"

"Yeah, he was one of those handsome TV doctors before your time. That new doctor makes me think of him. All tall, dark and handsome."

Shelby laughed. "Mrs. Stewart, you're outrageous." Mrs. Stewart's youngest son had to be older than Dr. Stiles. "You don't even know him and I really don't either. Anyway, he's only going to be helping out for a couple of weeks."

"Yeah, but you could have a little fun for a while. You're not dead. So stop acting like it."

Shelby patted the woman's arm. "For you I will try, I promise."

Without a doubt he had messed up this time. There had been no talking the judge out of his decision. Community service in a rural area. His lawyer had cautioned against arguing with the judge but Taylor had tried anyway. If he didn't have such a lead foot, he'd still be in Nashville in his nice modern trauma department instead of in a town like Benton. He'd run from a town similar to this one years ago and had never returned.

Taylor lifted the large-for-his-age two-year-old boy up onto the metal exam table. *Where in the world did you go to find a piece of medical office equipment from the 1950s?*

Thump, thump the table responded in rebellion as the boy's heels hit its side.

It was a sturdy table, Taylor would give it that.

The thin, frail mother carefully placed a brown bag she'd been carrying on the floor. She reminded Taylor of how his mother had looked when he had been a child, work weary and sad.

"So what's wrong with Greg?" Taylor looked at the boy's mother while keeping a hand on the wiggling child.

At one time he'd been like this little boy, dirty and wearing hand-me-down clothes from the church thrift closet. The sharp bite of memory froze him for a second. He pushed it aside. He hadn't dwelled on his dysfunctional childhood in years and he refused to start again today.

"I think he has something in his nose. We'll wait and let Doc Wayne take it out."

The mother doesn't trust me. Taylor didn't like that. He was the one with the knowledge who worked in a well-respected hospital, who had managed to get out of a nowhere town like this one, and she questioned his abilities. Turning away as if to get something, he gathered his patience.

Taylor faced the mother again. "Well, why don't I just take a quick look, okay?" Taylor forced his best smile for the mother then sought the otoscope that should have been hanging on the wall. "Uh, excuse me I need to find a light."

"There's a flashlight in the drawer." The mother pointed to the metal stand beside him.

Taylor pulled the drawer open and found what he needed, including plastic gloves. He checked inside the boy's nose. "There it is. In his left nostril. A lima bean, I believe. Do you mind if I get it out? Dr. Wayne will be busy for a while."

"I guess it'll be all right," the mother said without much enthusiasm.

"Let me find—"

"The big tweezers thing is in the jar on top of the stand," the mother said in a dry tone.

"So how often has Greg been in with this type of problem?" Taylor asked as he reached for the instrument in the outdated clear sterile jar.

"This is the third time in two weeks."

"Really. That often?" Taylor nodded his head thoughtfully. "Greg, you just lean back and hold still. I'll have that old bean out in no time," he said sternly enough so the boy would do as instructed but not so harshly as to scare him. The bean slipped out with a gentle tug and Taylor dropped it into the trash can, along with the gloves.

"Okay, young man, you're done here." Taylor picked up the boy and set him on his feet.

As if Taylor had pushed the button of a doorbell, the boy burst out crying then wailing. His slight mother hefted the child into her arms. "Shu, what's wrong, honey? Did the doctor hurt you?"

Great, now she's making the kid afraid of me.

"Sucker, I want a sucker," the child demanded between gasps.

Over the noise, Taylor asked, "Has Dr. Wayne been giving Greg a sucker each time she's taken something out of his nose?"

The woman nodded.

"Greg," Taylor said firmly, gaining the boy's attention and shutting off his tantrum. "If you don't put anything in your nose for one week then your mother will bring you by to get a sucker. Do you understand?"

The boy nodded his agreement and plopped his filthy thumb into his mouth.

"Good. See you next week."

As they exited the room the mother handed Taylor the brown sack she'd been carrying with extra care. "Your pay."

"Uh, thank you."

As the mother and child walked back down the hall toward the waiting area, Taylor unrolled the top of the bag. Nestled inside were six brown eggs. He crushed the top of the bag. He could remember his mother not being able to pay the doctor and bartering her house-cleaning services for medical care for him and his siblings. Of all the places the judge could have sent him, why did it have to be here?

"Where's my patient?" Dr. Wayne demanded as she looked around him into the room.

"He's gone."

"Gone where?"

"I examined him, and he's left."

Her shoulders went back, her chest came forward. He would've taken time to enjoy the sight if it hadn't been for her flashing gray eyes.

"That's not what I instructed you to do."

"I'm a doctor. I treated a patient. End of story."

She didn't say anything for a few moments. The blood rose in her face. More calmly than her appearance indicated she said, "We need to step into my office."

Turning, she walked to the end of the hallway. Apparently it wasn't until she reached the office door that she realized he hadn't moved. She glared at him.

Not appreciating being treated like a school child being called to the principal's office, Taylor resigned himself to putting up with her bossy ways for the time being. The judge had stated in no uncertain terms—clinic or jail.

"Coming, Dr. Wayne," he said, loud enough to be heard but with zero sincerity.

After he'd entered the office, she closed the flimsy door behind him. "Dr. Stiles, you will *not* come into my clinic six hours late and start doing as you please. If you'd been here on time I could've instructed you in the clinic protocol."

Straight chestnut hair that touched the ridge of her shoulders swayed as she spoke. Taylor would describe her as cute in a college co-ed sort of way. Her practical black slacks and white shirt did nothing to move her up on the looks scale.

"These are my people. I won't have you showing up for two short weeks and taking over. I cannot, will not, have you here for God knows what reason and let you destroy the trust I've built with my patients. I expect you to follow my instructions."

Who did this woman think she was, talking to him that way? Taylor carefully set the bag of eggs down on the desk. Turning his back to it, he placed his hands on the edge of the desk and leaned back.

"Doctor," he said, with enough disdain to make the word sound like he questioned whether or not that was the correct term. He took pleasure in watching the thrust of her breasts indicating her indignation as his barb struck home. "I won't be relegated to being your nurse. I'm the chief trauma doctor of a major hospital in Nashville. I can assure you that there will be few, if any, problems you see in this small, backwards clinic that I'll need your handholding for.

"I don't like being here any more than you obviously like having me. But what I can tell you is that I'm a good doctor. By no choice of my own, your patients are also *my* patients for the time being. Now, I suggest that we get back to that room full of people you're so concerned about."

Her mouth opened and closed. A sense of satisfaction filled him at having so thoroughly shut her up. Based on the last few minutes the next couple of weeks wouldn't be dull.

The infuriating doctor was calling his next patient before Shelby gathered her wits enough to follow him out of the office and down the hall. She'd never before forgotten about having patients waiting. It was a source of pride that she'd always put them first. Not even here a day and this egotistical doctor her uncle had sent had scrambled her brain. How was she supposed to survive the days ahead while having the likes of him in her face?

Who did he think he was talking to? The Benton Medical Clinic was hers. Her and Jim's dream. She'd make it clear later this evening who was in charge. For now she had to admit the high-handed doctor was right, she had patients to see.

The afternoon wore on and the most contact she had with Dr. Stiles was when they passed in the hall. It was narrow and their bodies brushed when they maneuvered by each other. For once she regretted not insisting that the landlord let her and Jim change the already existing partitions and make the hallway wider. Before they'd converted it to a medical clinic, the space had been an insurance company office without a large amount of traffic in the hallway.

The first time they passed each other her body went harp-string tight as a tingle rippled through her. She pushed it away, convincing herself it was a delayed reaction to being so irate with him. The next time he was too close was when he looked down at her with his dark steady gaze and said, "By the way, where's the nurse?"

"Don't have one. I have a teenager who's usually here but she's out sick today."

"Really," he said in astonishment. For a second she thought she saw admiration in his eyes. She wasn't sure why it mattered but she liked the thought that he might be impressed by something she did.

When he left her she felt like she'd just stepped out of a hot bath—all warm from head to toe. Thankfully she managed not to cross his path again.

Enough of those thoughts, Shelby scolded herself as she knelt to clean juice from the linoleum. The juice had spilt when a child had thrown a cup. Using a hand on her knee for balance, she pushed up and brushed her clothes off. Instead of her uniform of slacks and shirts she wished she could wear cute sundresses to work, but having to be the cleaning crew meant that wasn't practical.

She looked at the bright red car parked front and center of the door. Despite the fact the cost of it alone could finance the clinic for weeks, maybe months if she was thrifty, she'd love to climb into it and let her hair blow in the wind. Forget all her cares for a while. With a deep sigh she picked up the window cleaner. The trouble was, all her concerns would still be right here waiting. It was her responsibility to see that the clinic remained open.

Footfalls on the floor tiles drew her attention. Shelby moved out of the way so the last patient of the day could leave. "How're you, Mrs. Ferguson?" she asked the barrel-round woman with the white face.

"I would've been better if you hadn't been too busy to see me," she grumbled.

"How's that? Did Dr. Stiles not take good care of you?" The man was going to be out of here tonight if he'd upset Mrs. Ferguson.

"I don't like strange doctors looking me over," she groused.

Relieved there was nothing more to her concern than that, Shelby watched Taylor approach. As Mrs. Stewart had remarked, he was good looking but Shelby was more interested in his abilities, and those she couldn't question. He'd held up his end of the workload, she'd have to give him that. Most of the patients had been unsure about seeing him but had cautiously agreed when they'd been told how long they'd have to wait to see her. Most had given in and decided to let Taylor examine them. But there was a little part of Shelby that liked knowing she was their first choice.

"Dr. Stiles will only be helping out until the end of the month."

"Good," Mrs. Ferguson said, as she shifted her oversized bag on her ample hip. "Then things will get back to normal around here."

"So, are you two ladies talking about me?" Dr. Stiles came to stand beside them and flashed Mrs. Ferguson a grin.

Was there no end to the man's ego? "No." The word came out harsher than Shelby had intended, making her look guilty of doing exactly what he'd accused them of.

The twinkle in Taylor's eyes told her he knew it too. "Mrs. Ferguson, why don't I walk you out?"

She gave him a startled look. "Uh, I guess that would be all right." The woman clutched her purse in her sausage-sized fingers and shuffled towards the door.

Shelby made a swipe with the glass cleaner as she observed Taylor helping Mrs. Ferguson into her car. A summer breeze lifted the deep waves of his brown hair as he strolled back toward the clinic. Would it be soft and silky to the touch?

Shaking her head at thoughts like that, Shelby rubbed extra hard at a spot on the glass. It had been an easier day having Dr. Stile's help but she couldn't afford to get used to it. He wouldn't be there very long. Regardless of what good help he'd turned out to be, he made her angrier than anyone she'd ever known. She'd have a talk with him tonight and set the ground rules. This was her and Jim's clinic. She was in charge.

Shelby had stepped outside to wash the other side of the window by the time he'd reached the door. She glanced at him.

"Crusty old bird and a heart attack waiting to happen," he said, running a hand across his chin dark with stubble.

Suddenly she noticed the shadowy circles under his eyes. He looked tired. "I know. I've talked to her until I'm blue in the face. But she just can't bring herself to give up the carbs."

Shelby sprayed the window and began making circles with the rag. From the reflection in the glass she could tell the sun was turning pink in the western sky above the rolling hills and lush foliage of summer. She had to hurry or she wouldn't finish before she could no longer see.

"I'm bushed. I understand you have a place where I can stay," Taylor said as he pulled the door open.

"Yeah, but I have to finish up here before we leave."

"Don't you have a cleaning service?"

"Sure I do. Sometimes Carly, my receptionist, if she doesn't have a date. Which she almost always has." She glanced at him. He stood with his hands in his pockets and his head slanted in disbelief.

"Surely you don't do all the cleaning after seeing patients all day."

"Dr. Stiles—"

"Taylor. After hours I believe we can call each other by our first names."

Somehow it seemed petty not to agree. "Taylor, this is a state-supported clinic. And that may not last. Funding's tight and I have to constantly prove need. I'd rather put every dollar available into patient care."

Taylor looked through the glass at the room with the water-stained ceiling and mismatched chairs crowded against the wall. Shelby's voice spoke with pride but all he saw was a sad, needy place that he couldn't leave soon enough. It represented all that he had gladly left behind. He couldn't get back to his sparkling state-of-the-art hospital too soon. With a resigned breath he said, "Where do you keep the cleaning supplies?" He might as well help if he planned to get some sleep any time soon.

"Why?"

"I thought I'd help."

"I've got it."

Really, she was such a control freak that she even had to do all the cleaning? "It'll go twice as fast if I help."

"You're right. Stuff's in the closet in my office."

Taylor walked down the hall to the office and pulled the bucket full of cleaning materials out of the closet. The plastic pail was the same type his mother had carried when she'd cleaned people's homes. She had worked six days a week and even that hadn't always kept him and his two brothers in clothes or put food on the table. His drunken father...

"If you'll give me that, I'll do the restroom. I don't want you to mess up those pretty shoes," Shelby said.

"Oh, that's already happened. Little Jack Purdy threw up on them hours ago."

She wrinkled her nose. "Sorry."

"All part of the job. I'll sweep. Then can we get out of here."

"Yeah, I'll come in early and set up the rooms."

Was there anything she didn't do?

Thirty minutes later Shelby locked the door behind them and pulled the strap of her satchel over her slim shoulder. "Follow me."

He backed out of the parking space and was waiting before she'd made it to the ancient black pick-up across the three-row parking lot. He watched as Shelby pulled herself up into the truck. She was a petite woman, but she had a strong backbone to make up for any weakness she might have in other areas. A pit bull had nothing on her.

The whine of Shelby's starter refusing to co-operate and her hand hitting the steering-wheel told him he needed to offer her a lift. Taylor pulled in front of the truck. "Need a ride?"

She leaned out the open window. "Yeah, much as I hate to admit it."

"Is that riding with me you hate or that the truck won't start?"

"Both." She gave him a dry smile and climbed out of the truck, hefted her bag over her shoulder and came around the car.

He'd had no idea what to expect when the judge had ordered him here. He would've never imagined in a million years he'd find someone so smart, stubborn and surprisingly fascinating hiding out in some tiny 'burb in the middle of nowhere. Why was she here?

Taylor leaned across and unlatched the passenger door. Stretching farther, he pushed the door open. "Give me that." He pointed to the bag. Shelby handed it to him. "What've you got in this?" He put it in the space behind them.

"Charts." She slid into the low seat.

"You're taking work home? You've already put in, what? A twelve-hour day and now you're going to do paperwork. Don't you have a life?"

"The clinic is my life."

He gave her a long look. "I can see that."

She narrowed her eyes and said, "By the way, tomorrow please park away from the door. Leave the closer spaces for my patients. Some, like Mrs. Ferguson, can't walk very far."

He put up a hand. "Okay. I've been adequately rebuked. Which way?"

"Out of the lot and then to the left on the main road. My house isn't far."

That figured. She wouldn't live too far from her precious clinic. The only thing he'd ever been single-mindedly focused on had been getting the heck out of a town just like the one he was in now. Medicine had been the vehicle he'd used to achieve that goal. His lips twisted. Ironically, it had also been the vehicle that had brought him back.

"Turn to the left just past the white two-story house. My house is the third one on the right."

He pulled into the tree-lined street with perfect houses and immaculate lawns. The neighbors were out in the coolness of the evening. Two couples stood talking to each other while kids played nearby. At another house a man mowed his grass.

"True suburbia," Taylor murmured.

"Yes, it is and that's why I bought on this street.

I wanted to live where neighbors spoke to each other, helped each other. Where children could play and be safe."

His stomach clinched. The scene she described was everything he'd ever dreamed of as a kid. Slowly releasing a breath, he pulled his car into the paved drive Shelby indicated. The house was a red-brick ranch style with a two-story detached wooden garage and stairs running along the outside.

"You'll be staying there." Shelby pointed at the garage when he turned off the car engine.

"I'm staying here?" If working in the makeshift clinic wasn't bad enough, staying in this homey neighborhood might kill him. "With you?"

"You're not staying *with* me. I rent this out. It just happens I don't have a tenant right now."

Things had just got more interesting.

She glanced over her shoulder to the neighbors watching from across the street, then turned to him and grinned. "You've already started the neighbors talking. We don't often see cars like this in Benton."

"I guess you don't." Taylor felt his lips thin. He didn't like being talked about. He'd spent his youth being the topic of gossip, being made fun of. At least these people weren't talking about him in relationship to the town drunk.

Her smile had disappeared by the time his gaze met hers. "You know, if you don't want people to notice you then you might try not living so extravagantly." She opened the door and climbed out, picking up her satchel.

How had she read him so well? Were his feelings that obvious? He'd spent years learning to hide them. How had this woman he known mere hours been able to see through him?

Taylor stepped out of the car and slammed the door, facing her. "Extravagantly?" His voice rose. "I'll have you know I work hard for what I have. I can afford this car and I don't have to justify it to you or anyone else."

"Little touchy, aren't you?" she replied with a noticeable effort to keep her voice down.

"Everything okay, Shelby?" a deep voice called.

Taylor glared at the man who had crossed the street to stand at the end of her drive. Small towns never changed. People were always in your business.

She walked a few steps toward the man and waved. "Everything's fine, Mr. Marshall. I'm just showing Dr. Stiles where he'll be staying while he's in town."

Taylor went to the trunk of the car, popped it and grabbed his suitcase.

"Okay," Mr. Marshall said. "We'll see you at the block party, won't we?"

"Sure. Looking forward to it."

"Bring the new doctor along if you wish. We'd like to meet him."

Taylor certainly hoped that she wasn't planning on him attending any party. The Arctic would become a beach before he'd attend any social function around here. He'd made himself into an arts and opera guy. Benton didn't even have a movie theater, from what he could tell.

Shelby turned, her gray eyes flashing, her tone tight with control. "Don't you ever raise your voice to me again where my neighbors can hear. They worry about me."

She motioned towards the garage stairs and headed that way. "You'll not come here and upset them or create fodder for talk at their dinner tables. For some reason I don't understand, Uncle Gene thinks I'm a halfway house warden for bad-boy trauma doctors." The last few words were said more to herself than to him.

So, Shelby didn't like being the talk of the town any more than he did. Maybe they had more in common than he'd given her credit for.

CHAPTER TWO

SHELBY dropped her bag on the bottom step of the stairs that ran alongside the garage.

"Since you don't want to be a topic of gossip any more than I do," Taylor said calmly, "maybe you should just agree to disagree about my car."

With great effort Shelby pushed down the temptation to say something. Having a public argument would certainly give her neighbors and friends a good tale to tell.

"Just what did you do to get on Uncle Gene's bad side?"

"Uncle Gene?" he asked in a puzzled tone.

"Judge Gene Robbins. He's my uncle," she said as she started to climb the stairs.

"So that's why I'm here." The words were little more than a mumble, as if he was contemplating the meaning of life. After a moment he commented, "We've had a few legal dealings. Nothing special."

Shelby stopped and looked down at him. What

did he mean? Was he an ax murderer? No, her uncle wouldn't send anyone to work with her who wasn't a decent person.

Taylor's look moved slowly up from where his focus had been, on her bottom. Heat filled her cheeks. It had been a long time since a man had noticed her and made his appreciation so obvious. She and Jim had been an item since childhood, leaving little room for another man to show interest. The men in Benton had never approached her in anything other than friendship since Jim had been gone. In truth, she'd not given them a chance. She couldn't take the chance of losing someone she loved again.

Shelby hurried up the stairs. Taylor was here to help in the clinic and that was all. On the landing she opened the door to the apartment.

"You don't lock up?"

Turning round, she found Taylor too close for comfort. Standing on the small landing that made her a step higher than he, Shelby was almost at eye level with him.

From there she could see the tiny laugh lines that radiated out from the corners of his eyes. Apparently he wasn't always the hypercritical person his body language indicated he was. His eyes were brown with small flakes of gold.

The twist of the corner of his mouth brought her attention to his firm, full lips. She blinked.

"Doesn't your husband tell you to lock the doors?" he asked.

"I'm a widow."

"I'm sorry." He sounded like he meant it.

"I am too." She turned away from the sincerity in his eyes. The sadness that usually accompanied thoughts of Jim was suddenly not as sharp.

Shelby hadn't missed the look of displeasure on Taylor's face when he had entered the clinic or when he'd seen the working conditions. She'd also not missed the expression of disgust when he'd realized she drove an old truck. His knuckles had turned white on his steering-wheel when he'd pulled onto her street, as if he didn't like her neighborhood. Did he think that living here was beneath him? Or was it that she rubbed him the wrong way?

"How does your family feel about you being away from home?" she asked.

"No family." He made it sound like he liked it that way.

Entering the one-room apartment, Shelby

moved to one side to prevent any physical contact. He made her feel nervous and she was never nervous around men. After dropping his bag on the floor, he looked around the place.

Shelby's gaze followed his. A full bed with her grandmother's hand-quilted blanket dominated the room. There was a small refrigerator-stove combo in one corner. A two-seater table with chairs sat in front of the double window that looked out onto the back of her house. A braided rug, sofa and chair finished off the living area. A bathroom took up the other corner. She was rather pleased with her decorating efforts. It made a cute place for one person to stay.

"I think you will be comfortable here," she said with a smile full of pride.

He didn't agree or disagree. Instead he picked up his bag, carried it to the bed and began unzipping it.

"Not up to your usual standards, I'm sure," she mumbled.

Taylor pulled clothing out of his bag, his back to her. "You don't know me well enough to know my standards. Now, if you'll excuse me, I'm going to get a much-needed shower and go to bed. I've been up almost twenty-four hours."

"What? Why?"

"Because I had to handle an emergency last night. A boy had been hit by a car. I didn't get out of the hospital until ten this morning and then I had to drive straight here or *Uncle Gene* would've been unhappy."

So that's why he'd been late. Why hadn't she noticed he wasn't just tired, he was exhausted? As a physician trained to observe the human condition she should've known. Had she completely missed it because of her strange reaction to his nearness?

Now she felt small and petty. Why hadn't he said something? She could've given him directions here. The clinic had been running with just her for three years and she could've certainly made it through another afternoon. Instead, Taylor had gone to work, never giving the patients or her any indication he was drained. His perfect bedside manner had never faltered. For that, he'd earned her admiration.

Taylor began unbuttoning his dress shirt.

Shelby headed for the door but turned back when she reached it. "One more thing about the clinic…" Her gaze went to where his hands worked the buttons open.

"Yeah?"

His shirt parted, revealing a broad chest lightly covered with dark hair. Her gaze rose to meet his. One of his dark brows rose quizzically.

Heaven help her, she'd been caught staring. Shelby drew in a quick breath. "Uh, do you mind keeping your clothes on until I'm gone?"

"Actually, I do. Can't whatever you have to say wait?"

Was she losing her mind? She didn't stand around in half-naked strangers' rooms. Holding her ground, she gave him her best piercing look. "No. I need to make a few things clear before tomorrow."

"Go ahead. I guess I can't stop you," he said as he shrugged out of his shirt and let it drop to the floor.

"Although I appreciate your help today, it needs to be clear to the patients that I'm in charge. I make the decisions. I determine what the patients require. I will not have you changing routines I've worked hard to implement. Is that clear?"

"So, to make it short and sweet, you're the boss."

Put that way, he made her sound like a shrew. That didn't sit well. "It's just that—"

He put up a hand, halting her words. "I've got it. Now, if you'll excuse me, I'd like to get some shut-eye."

Departing, she carried the feeling she'd been the one reprimanded. "The clinic opens at eight sharp," she said over her shoulder.

"I'll be there."

Taylor woke to threads of early morning sunshine through the window. He'd slept well, whether from exhaustion or because this simple room had offered him a good mattress he didn't know.

Shelby had been right. He didn't think much of the apartment but on second look it did have a rather homey feel. It was a great deal nicer than what he'd had growing up. To even have a bed to himself would've been considered high living.

He glanced at the electric clock on the bedside table. It said seven twenty-eight. The woman would have his hide if he didn't turn up on time this morning. He couldn't take a chance that she'd inform her Uncle Gene about his tardiness. More time he couldn't do.

Ten minutes later, freshly shaven and dressed in khakis, a knit shirt and loafers, he opened the door and almost stepped in the tray sitting on the stoop. There he found a Thermos of coffee, toast and a boiled egg. He smiled. Maybe the caustic doctor was feeling a little guilty about how she'd treated him when he'd been late. Apparently she wasn't all vinegar.

He checked the time. If he didn't get a move on she might chew him out again. Grabbing the Thermos and egg, he closed the door behind him and hurried down the stairs. Knocking on the back door of her house, he received no response. She must've found a ride to work. If she wasn't at the clinic when he got there, he'd hunt for her.

As Taylor walked across the parking lot towards the clinic, Shelby came out. "Coming in under the wire, aren't you, Doctor?" Her voice was full of censure as she worked the key until the deadbolt was drawn into the door to open the office for the day.

"I said I'd be here, and I'm here. And good morning to you too, Doctor. What time did you show up?"

"I've been here an hour or so. It usually takes me that long to set up for the day."

"I knocked to see if you needed a ride."

"I walked. Bert said he'd have my truck fixed this afternoon."

Taylor held the door for her to enter ahead of him. "You walked? I would've brought you if you'd woken me."

"You were tired. Walking isn't a problem. I do it pretty regularly. I'm safe enough and it's good exercise."

A couple of people who'd been waiting around outside came in behind them.

"Thanks for the breakfast." He showed her the egg and Thermos.

"No problem. Those'll have to wait, though. We've patients to see."

Her no-nonsense statement went along with her functional attire of navy slacks and white V-neck T-shirt that showed a hint of cleavage. Despite her simple attire, it couldn't hide the shapely curves of her body. Her waist was small enough that a man's hands could easily slip around it.

She'd pulled her hair back but at the nape it was too short to capture. The only flash of color was a bright neon-pink stethoscope hanging around her neck. Taylor followed her to the desk, where a blonde teenage girl sat, drumming a pencil and chewing gum.

"Carly, this is Dr. Stiles. He'll be helping us

for the next couple of weeks," Shelby said as she picked up the sign-in clipboard.

Taylor nodded to the girl.

She looked up. He watched her eyes widen. She shifted, then straightened in her chair. "Hey." She flipped her long blonde hair behind her shoulder. He'd never thought of himself as vain, far from it, but he did know when a female appreciated his looks.

"Carly, do you think you could find Ms. Cooper's file? And get rid of the gum." Shelby turned to him, "I'll see Ms. Cooper since this is a checkup."

Carly didn't move. He didn't know why but he wished Shelby would have the same reaction to him that Carly did. Other than that one unguarded moment when he'd been unbuttoning his shirt, she'd acted as if she had no idea he was male. It intrigued and disappointed him. Simple admiration from Shelby would be hard earned.

"I'll call Dr. Stiles's patient for him," Carly said as she dropped her gum into the trash can at her feet and gave him a toothy smile.

"Will I be using exam one?" he asked Shelby.

"That'll be fine."

Her words were said so tersely that he glanced at her. What was her problem now?

For the rest of the morning he had little time to ponder what might have upset Shelby. The waiting room stayed full no matter how efficiently he tended to the patients or how simple the cases were.

Where Carly's reaction to him had been an ego booster earlier in the day, it had become borderline comical by mid-day. He noticed that she saw to all his patients, showing them to their exam room, asking him if he had everything he needed or if she could get him something to drink. All of it was nice but it was in direct contrast to how Carly treated Shelby. Carly offered her no assistance.

When Taylor asked Carly about that she shrugged in a typical teenage dramatic fashion and said, "Oh, Dr. Wayne likes to do everything herself."

Of course she does.

By lunchtime Taylor couldn't help but admit that he'd put in a pretty hard morning. The little clinic was plenty busy. The mundane work sucked him back to another time. Each patient reminded him too much of the people he'd known growing up.

There was the kid with the cough that never disappeared, like Mike Walker's. He'd been in Taylor's third-grade class one year but wasn't there the next. Or others, such as old man Parsons, who'd had no teeth and had chewed tobacco until his gums were diseased. Or Mrs. Roberts, who might've been pretty at fifty, but with too many children and a sorry husband had looked like she was seventy.

Taylor would do his time and get back to where he belonged, where memories weren't darts being thrown at him constantly.

Around noon the egg he'd eaten in bites between patients was gone. He was glad to see that the crowd in the waiting room had dwindled. Maybe they would let him and Shelby have some lunch before every seat was filled again.

"Where do you get a good burger in this town?" Taylor asked as Shelby approached the front desk.

"There's a burger place on Main," Carly offered.

"We can all go. I'll buy," he offered.

Shelby gave a negative shake of her head. "I

have paperwork to do. And someone may come in." She slipped a chart into the file cabinet.

Really? The woman couldn't even stop long enough to go out for a quick bite of lunch?

"I want to go. Can we ride in that cool car of yours?"

Taylor wasn't sure he wanted to be seen riding around town with the very young girl beside him but there was no choice because he had no idea where the burger joint was and he was starving. "Can we bring you back something?" Taylor asked Shelby.

"No, I have a pack of crackers in my desk."

"Okay." He shrugged. "But I bet a burger would be a lot better." He looked at Carly. "Come on. Show me the way. I guess I should learn my way around town."

Shelby pulled out the drawer of her desk and reached for the package of crackers but didn't pick them up. She would've been satisfied with them if Taylor hadn't mentioned a burger.

She popped the top of her diet drink and stared off into space. The sounds of Carly's high-pitched giggle and Taylor's deep rumble came from the front. It grew louder as they walked in her direction.

Taylor stopped and let Carly enter Shelby's office before him. "We decided to go through the drive-in and pick up something. We brought you a burger. Before you argue, I owe you for breakfast and the place to stay."

Carly's eyes widened with surprise. "You're staying at Doc Wayne's?"

"Yeah." Taylor pulled one of the spare chairs closer to the desk with his foot.

Carly looked from Taylor to Shelby and back to Taylor.

No telling what the rumor would be if she didn't clear this up now. "He's staying in my garage apartment."

"Oh, I thought—"

"I know what you thought." Shelby said in a tight voice.

Already this man was disrupting her life. Carly would have that information spread far and wide by the end of the day.

Maybe Uncle Gene could have sent her someone else less... She couldn't think of the word. Intrusive? Disruptive? Attractive?

Taylor sat down in one of the two folding chairs

that suddenly appeared child-size beneath his large body and started digging through the paper bag in his hand. He acted as if he took his meals in a tiny, shabby office every day. It didn't take long for Taylor to act like he belonged. Carly took the other chair and he handed her a burger wrapped in paper before his hand slipped into the bag again. Pulling out another burger, he offered it to Shelby.

When she hesitated he said, "Take it. Don't act like you don't want it."

Shelby wished that wasn't the truth. She reached for the offered package. By the time she'd eaten a couple of bites of hers Taylor had already finished his first burger and was searching the bag for another.

The tinkle of the bell hanging on the door sounded.

"Doc Wayne! Doc Wayne!"

The urgent cry made Shelby stand and head towards the door. Taylor had hurried out and was moving up the hall by the time she stepped from the office.

The metallic smell of blood reached her nose before she saw the bright red drops on the floor. It seeped through the rag wrapped around Mr. Hardy's arm. Shelby's stomach rolled like a boat on a stormy sea, making her wish she hadn't eaten.

She mentally braced herself. She could do this.

"Sir," Taylor said, "I'm Dr. Stiles. Come back to the exam room and we'll see what we've got here."

For once Shelby was glad to have Taylor take over. When the injured man, in his mid-fifties, gave her a questioning look she said, "He's a trauma doctor. You're in good hands."

Shelby believed those words. Was it because of the way Taylor led with confidence or because of the quality of care she'd seen him provide? Either way, it kept her from having to deal with the blood.

"Carly," she called, "get out a suture kit in exam one. Now." She turned to the pale-faced woman left standing in the waiting room. Shelby took her arm and led her to a chair.

"Wait here, Mrs. Hardy. We'll let you see him as soon as we can."

Shelby headed toward the exam room. "Carly, get Mrs. Hardy a drink and sit with her. She looks a little shaken," Shelby said as she passed the girl in the hall.

In the examination room, Taylor gingerly unwrapped the rag from around the man's arm. Stepping to the table, she asked, "Mr. Hardy, what did you do to yourself?"

"I was cutting a limb off a tree that'd been damaged during the storm last week. Darn chainsaw kicked back and got me."

Shelby took a fortifying breath as Taylor revealed the gnarled flesh on Mr. Hardy's forearm. She'd never been a fan of blood to start with but after seeing so much of Jim's pouring from his body, her aversion to it had become worse. Red liquid continued to slowly drip onto the white cloth covering the table. "Looks like it got you three times before it let go," Taylor remarked as he examined the man's arm. "I don't see any bone damage."

"Do you mind if I have a look?" Shelby asked, stepping forward. Cases like these were her least favorite but she'd learned to deal with them because she was usually the only doctor available. She wouldn't let this know-it-all doctor make her look weak in front of a patient who would be hers long after he'd gone home.

Taylor shifted to the right so she could have a better view. Shelby gently rotated the arm. "Does that hurt?" Her stomach chose that moment to make a Waikiki surfing wave. She hoped her face didn't give away to Mr. Hardy and Taylor how awful she felt.

"No," the middle-aged man said.

She gently eased the man's arm down on the table. Her hands trembled and she tightened her jaw, willing her throat not to spasm. If she focused on what she was doing, she could get through it. She had before and she would again. "Well, I don't see any damage past the skin, which is good news. We just need to get you stitched up."

Something made her look at Taylor. He was studying her too closely for her comfort. Seconds later a look of realization entered his dark expressive eyes then surprise.

"Dr. Wayne," he said, his tone all business, "do you mind if I do the suturing? It's my expertise and I don't see many chainsaw injuries where I'm from."

A sense of relief washed over her. She looked at Mr. Hardy questioningly.

"I don't mind. Just need to get it done. My wife's already mad 'cos I got blood all over her freshly mopped kitchen floor."

The bell on the door sounded and Carly spoke

to someone. "If you have this," Shelby said to Taylor, "I'll go see this other patient."

Taylor glanced up at Mr. Hardy, "We're good here?"

The man nodded agreement. Shelby left as Taylor untaped the suture kit.

Over an hour later Shelby stood beside the front desk ready to call her next patient. She watched as Taylor saw Mr. and Mrs. Hardy out with instructions to return in a couple of days.

Taylor approached the desk and stepped close enough she could smell the soap on his skin that she'd placed in his bath. "We need to talk."

A shiver ran up her spine. "Is something wrong with Mr. Hardy?"

"Your office," he said in a low voice.

"You don't order me around."

"Do you really want to broadcast our discussion to the entire county?" He turned his back to the handful of people in the waiting room. "I don't think you want people to know their doctor's little secret."

Her stomach dropped. He wasn't going to let what he'd learned pass without comment. She entered the office ahead of him. He came in and closed the door.

"What've you got to say that can't wait until after our patients are gone?" she demanded.

Taylor leaned causally against the door, crossing his arms over his chest and one foot over the other, a slight grin on his lips. "Interesting, a doctor who can't stand the sight of blood," he stated in complete amazement.

"I'm a general practitioner. I don't have to deal with blood to do my job well," she huffed.

"I guess you don't. But you must've had a devil of a time getting through emergency rotation in med school."

She looked him directly in the eyes. "I worked through it."

"Yeah, I could see how well you're working through it in there with Mr. Hardy." He had to admire her fortitude. She looked as if she was determined to do what had to be done, even at a cost to herself.

"You won't tell, will you?"

He wished he could tease her and make her think that he would but her wide-eyed, pleading look softened his heart. "Your secret is safe with me."

"You know, I would've stitched up Mr. Hardy if you hadn't been here. Wouldn't have enjoyed it but I would've gotten it done. Patients with major injuries don't normally come to the clinic. His wife refusing to drive outside Benton is the only reason they stopped here. Otherwise they would've gone straight to Nashville or Jackson."

"Either one of those places is around a hundred miles away."

"I know. Mr. Hardy could've gone into shock before he got there."

Shelby gave him a grateful look that made him feel heroic. "I appreciate your help."

The frustration she felt over her weakness shone in her large gray eyes. The desire to take her in his arms and reassure her that she wasn't failing her patients flooded him. Taylor resisted the urge. Shelby wouldn't appreciate him noting her flaw any more than he'd already had. He shrugged. "I'm glad I was here too. The old man required a number of stitches."

Taylor had actually found Mr. Hardy's case interesting. Chainsaw accidents weren't common inside a metropolitan area. To his surprise, he'd enjoyed talking to the tell-it-like-it-is man. Straightening, Taylor prepared to open the door. "I did some of my finest work. He'll have scars but nothing as extensive as they could've been."

"Well, I'm glad it worked out for you *and* Mr. Hardy," Shelby said in a mocking tone.

She made it sound as if Taylor had caused the accident so he could show off his skills. At least that sad expression had left her eyes. He ignored her remark and asked, "So what's the plan when I'm gone?"

"The plan is to go on as I have been and look for a doctor who's trained in emergency medicine. Someone willing to work here at least part time."

"Well, it won't be me. I'm going to do what's required. Then I'm gone. Don't be getting any ideas."

"I don't have any ideas about you one way or another. Uncle Gene said he was sending me some help for a couple of weeks. The minute I met you I knew you wouldn't be staying long."

He didn't understand why that remark annoyed him. He didn't like her thinking she knew him that well. "Why?"

"Well, let's see," she said with a sassy bob to her head, "car, clothes, attitude. All are a dead giveaway."

He'd covered his past well. Had worked hard at it. Taylor stepped closer, stopping just outside her personal space. Her eyes shifted with apprehension. He made her nervous and he liked it.

Leaning down to her eye level, he said, "You of all people should know that appearances aren't always how things are." He paused. "For example, a doctor who hates the sight of blood."

A knock on the door punctuated his statement.

"It's standing room only out here," Carly called.

"Maybe you'd better go do what you have to do," Shelby said in an ice-cold voice as she moved past him to hold open the door.

Taylor spent Wednesday morning seeing patients, only able to snatch a quick lunch before the afternoon influx of people into the waiting room. Despite working in a small-town clinic, he was still keeping large trauma center hours. It amazed him that Shelby had managed to hold it together without help for so long. She had to be mentally and physically exhausted. The clinic was definitely a two-person set-up, and three would be better.

Late that afternoon, Taylor trailed behind his latest patient as he left. Going to the front to call his next one, he was pleasantly surprised to find that there was no one else needing attention. Shelby was busy giving Carly directions and shifting through papers at the same time. The picture had become so commonplace it seemed like he'd been working at the Benton Clinic for ever. It amazed him that he didn't feel more like an outsider.

He and Shelby had only spoken a few words to each other the entire day. For some reason, he'd missed their sparring. If nothing else it brought a little spark to the backwater town, something to challenge his mind.

The bell on the door rang. The peace hadn't lasted long enough for him to even say something that would aggravate Shelby. A girl of around sixteen with large, gloomy eyes and long blonde hair entered looking as if she'd like to turn and run. She wore a simple dress covering too much of her body for the warm day. The girl hesitated as the door closed behind her.

Shelby must have realized that the three of them looking at the girl was intimidating because she stepped forward and offered her hand. "I'm Dr. Wayne. Can I help you?"

The girl nodded but didn't make eye contact.

"Come this way." Shelby led the teen down the hall.

Ten minutes later Taylor entered the small lab

area to find Shelby facing the counter, gripping it so hard the veins on the top of her hands stood out. She kept her head down.

He closed the door. "What's wrong?" he asked, keeping his voice low and stepping closer. "What's happened?" He didn't try to keep his concern out of his voice.

Shelby's actions seemed out of character. Even when blood had been an issue she'd hung tough, but now...

"Nothing." Her tone said differently.

"Something's obviously wrong. Let me help."

She turned so quickly that she caught him off guard. Her eyes glistened and her face was drawn with misery. "Really? You think you can help," she muttered. "I have an unwed pregnant teen in there..." she gestured toward the door across the hall "...who's terrified to talk to her parents. When she does find the courage to tell her family about the baby she also has to explain to them that she has a venereal disease. So just how can you help with this?"

Her bold stare said he couldn't fix this no matter what he did. As much as he hated to admit it, she was right.

"I can't help her but I can help you." He gathered Shelby into his arms. What was he doing? Nurses, other female doctors had been upset in his presence and he'd never hugged them. Something about Shelby made him want to comfort her, help her with her problems. Be there for her. He winced. That was something he couldn't do. How had he become so involved in her life so quickly?

She resisted, remaining rigid against him. "Please let me go."

It pricked his ego that she wouldn't consent to his comfort, but he schooled his face not to show a reaction. He did as she asked and stepped back, missing the contact immediately. "Would you like me to talk to the girl?"

Shelby shook her head. "No, that's my job. She's scared enough without me sending a man in to discuss this. She lives in the county above us and wanted to go where she wouldn't be recognized. Someone told her that there was a female doctor here."

"In this day and age she's hiding? Afraid to tell her parents? The teenage girls I know are proud to be unwed and pregnant."

"You have to remember that there're still strong

moral standards in this area. Everyone knows everyone. Has an opinion about everything."

Taylor was well aware of how those concepts worked.

Shelby continued, "Her parents, she says, aren't going to be happy or accepting." She moved past him. "I'd better go give her the news."

He placed a hand on her shoulder and her gaze met his. "Shelby, I wish I could do more than say I'm sorry."

She gave him a weak smile. "I am too," she said, before squaring her shoulders and knocking on the door to the exam room across the hall.

Her heart was too big for her own good. For once, Taylor thought that Uncle Gene sentencing him to the clinic had been a good thing. It had allowed him to be there for Shelby today.

The girl left the clinic thirty minutes later with a gentle pat on the shoulder from Shelby and the reassurance that she'd be there if the girl needed her. Shelby said not a word as she passed him. She entered her office and effectively closed everyone out.

After preparing the clinic for the next day, Taylor knocked lightly on the office door. "You ready to close up?"

"You go on. I'll see you in the morning."

She needed space and wouldn't appreciate him insisting she leave. He really shouldn't care. All doctors ran into cases that got under their skin. The problem was that Shelby cared too deeply. For the girl. For her all her patients.

Who took care of her?

Hours later, Taylor rolled over in bed and looked at the bedside clock for the umpteenth time. It was well past midnight.

Where was she?

With a sense of relief that amazed him he saw Shelby's headlights flash across the wall of the apartment as she pulled into the drive.

She worked far too hard, felt too much. The clinic, for all he could see, was her life. She took no down time. In his opinion it wasn't healthy. She needed to slow down or she'd be the one needing a doctor. He knew of few doctors who worked harder than Shelby.

He didn't want to care. No matter what happened he refused to get involved but with every day he stayed in Benton it made it more difficult to keep his distance. First it had been Mrs. Ferguson, then Mr. Hardy and now he was stressing about a workaholic tyrant of a doctor who lived in a one-red-light town. Heck, he didn't really know how to care. He'd certainly not gotten an example of how that worked from his family. Could he have picked a more foreign emotion?

The way Shelby's big gray eyes looked stormy when she was mad and turned soft and sad when she worried over a patient pulled at him. Even her sharp tongue didn't squelch his anxiety for the turbocharged woman.

Reassured Shelby was safely home, Taylor rolled over and punched his pillow, knowing he could now find sleep. He'd no idea why it mattered to him what she did. Shelby had been fine before he'd arrived and she'd be fine after he left.

But who would be there for her when she needed a shoulder to lean on next time?

CHAPTER THREE

THURSDAY evening Shelby pulled into her drive well after dark. She'd stayed late at the clinic to finish some charting. Now her plan was to spend the next few hours working on grant applications. She had to find some long-term help for the clinic soon or the state would shut it down. Taylor had made it abundantly clear he wouldn't be the answer to her problem.

The old truck rattled to a stop when Shelby shut it off. She regarded the sports car in front of her. She'd always liked nice cars but her parents were supportive but practical people who didn't encourage that type of extravagance. Shelby couldn't really see herself ever owning such a fancy vehicle. She was the wrong type of doctor, in the wrong area of the world, to even drive one. Still, a girl could appreciate a nice ride.

A movement in the garage window caught her attention. Taylor stood silhouetted there. He wore no shirt and was talking on the phone. Shelby's attention was riveted to his wide shoulders that tapered to a trim waist. Sliding down in the seat, she hoped he wouldn't see her and think she'd already gone into the house. His pants rode low on his hips. He must work out. A lot. She'd say his efforts were worth it.

Frustration welled within her. She had no business even noticing him. There could never be anything real between them. She had to keep reminding herself of that. He wasn't staying and she refused to care then be hurt when he left. She'd barely lived through that pain before and she couldn't do it again.

Taylor put a hand above his head and stretched. Shelby sucked in a breath. Good heavens. Her heart went into overdrive. Ignoring him was going to be much more difficult than she imagined. The tingle of desire that had lay dormant since Jim's death had returned, heating her from the inside out, catching her by surprise. She needed to go into the house. Stand under the air-conditioning vent. Her reaction to this well-built man was way over the top.

How would she get inside without looking like she'd become a peeping Tomette? She grinned. At least she hadn't lost her sense of humor even though she'd lost her mind. With relief, and disappointment she didn't want to examine, Taylor moved away from the window.

Gathering her bag, she opened the truck door and slid out. Closing the door with less force than usual, she accused herself of being silly. This was her house, her drive, her neighborhood. Seeing Taylor Stiles's chest from a distance wasn't that big a deal. She'd even seen it up close. As a doctor she'd seen all kinds of half-naked men.

Yeah, but chests as fine as Taylor's were few and far between. Great. Now she was starting to think like Carly. Lifting her shoulders and standing taller, Shelby walked to the back door. Why hadn't she left the porch light on?

"I was wondering how long it would take you to get out of the truck."

Shelby jumped, dropping her bag. "What're you doing, sneaking up on me?"

"I wasn't sneaking. I came down the stairs like I always do. Your mind must've been on something else."

Thankful for the shadows, she didn't want to contemplate what her mind had been on and she certainly didn't need him to see the guilt covering her face.

"I wanted to speak to you a minute," Taylor said.

Shelby retrieved her bag. "Could we make it quick? I'm really not up for some long discussion right now. All I want is a sandwich and to get to bed early."

"Why don't you get that sandwich while we talk?" He followed her up the steps. "I wouldn't mind having one too."

She reached inside and flipped on the light switches for the kitchen and the outside. Glancing around at him, she was relieved to find he'd pulled on a T-shirt before coming out to meet her. "Do you make it a habit of inviting yourself into people's homes? To meals? Anyway, I thought you finally agreed to go to Vinnie's with Carly and her boyfriend. I heard her begging you to go."

"That was hours ago. I've a pretty big appetite."

Suddenly hers was gone. Her mouth went dry. Her mind was going places it shouldn't. That she didn't want it to go.

"Shelby?"

"Huh?"

"Aren't you going inside?"

Shelby opened the screen door and entered the

kitchen, dropping her bag in one of the kitchen chairs. Taylor followed her.

"Hey, I still didn't say you could come in."

"Awe, come on, Shelby. Have pity on a hungry man with nothing in his pantry. Share a sandwich."

With a sigh, she said, "Okay, one sandwich and tell me what you need, then you're out of here."

The large family kitchen shrank, taking on a more intimate feel with Taylor in it. To cover her unease, Shelby gathered the sandwich fixings. Having Taylor in her home made them seem like more than colleagues. Maybe friends? In just a few short days. Could a woman be just friends with someone who exuded all-male sex-appeal as Taylor did? No, she needed to protect herself. He'd never settle here and she'd never be someone's two-week stand.

Placing the bread, ham, cheese and condiments on the table, Shelby poured two glasses of iced tea. She set Taylor's glass before him, taking special care not to touch him. Taking the chair opposite him, she reached for the bread. Her hand circled the mustard bottle at the same time his did. His fingers brushed across hers. Their warmth against the coolness of hers made her shiver. She let the bottle go but Taylor's touch lingered.

"Ladies first," he quipped, going after the cheese instead.

A sense of disgust filled her. She was acting like a ninny and he wasn't even affected. After her meltdown the other day, he probably wasn't surprised by the way she acted.

Taking a sip of tea, she carefully set the glass down and finished making her sandwich. She'd never let him know that even his casual touch rattled her. She took a restorative breath and said, "So what do you want to talk about?"

"I was wondering if the clinic is open on the weekends. I have a date for the opera in Nashville and need to know if I should cancel it."

It shouldn't have surprised her that Taylor might have a love interest back home but until then she'd not given it any thought. He'd said there was no family but that didn't mean he didn't have someone special waiting for his return. One he obviously missed. A girlfriend. The prick of rejection caught her unawares. Why should she feel that way? There wasn't anything between them.

"The clinic's open on Saturday from eight to

noon. After that the weekend is yours. I'll expect you there at eight on Monday morning sharp."

"Yes, ma'am. Do you know how often you use the word 'expect'?" he asked around a bite of ham sandwich. It wasn't said as a putdown but more as a conversational question.

"I don't use it a lot," she said with a huff.

"Yeah, you do," he said nonchalantly as he looked over her head. "Nice pictures."

A swell of pride filled her at his compliment. "They were some of my husband's favorites." She'd been able to capture the essence of her subjects in the photos, showing the truth of what life was like in this rural area.

"His favorite photographer?"

"You could say that. Me."

"Really? You took these?" Taylor stood, moving closer to study the two lines of framed photographs, six pictures in all. "You really caught what the subjects were feeling. I'm impressed."

"Thanks." A warm glow filled her at his compliment. "Those are really old. I don't have time to take pictures now." She picked up her sandwich.

"Why's that?" He took his chair again, propping his elbows on the table and giving her his full attention.

Her hand tightened on her sandwich. Having his intent look focused on her made her feel self-conscious. "Well, I have the clinic to run."

"So what's the deal with the clinic? I'd think you could have your choice of positions anywhere you'd like."

Shelby pushed away the plate holding her half-eaten sandwich. "I want to work here. The clinic was our dream."

His brows rose. "'Our'?"

"Mine, and my husband's." To her surprise the stab of pain she normally felt when she spoke of Jim wasn't as strong as it had once been.

Taylor prompted, "So you and your husband started the clinic?"

"We grew up together. Jim wanted to be a doctor and I did too. So we decided to go to medical school together and work where we were needed the most, which was here. It might be a small town, but it needed medical help and we could provide that, *wanted* to provide that."

"Well, I'm glad there are doctors like you because I couldn't do this."

"Do what?"

"Live here."

Her chair made a scraping noise as she pushed away from the table. Indignation and the need to defend Benton welled up in her. She stood and picked up her plate. "I can appreciate that Benton might not be for everyone but I happen to love living here. I love the town square with our wonderful old courthouse. I love the shops and the fact that the store owners call me by name when I go in. I love that we have no traffic!" She looked pointedly at him. "What I don't appreciate is people coming here and insulting it."

"I'm not insulting your precious town," Taylor said, following her. His arm brushed hers as he placed his plate in the sink.

A ripple of awareness went up her arm and ran through her body. She stepped out of reach, not liking the out-of-control feeling she had when he was near.

"I'm just saying living here isn't for me," Taylor continued, as if nothing had happened.

For him, she guessed it hadn't. "You know, I think it's time for you to go. I'm going to call it a night."

Taylor stepped to the door. "I'll see you in the morning."

At the slap of the screen door closing, loneliness filled her. The large country kitchen suddenly seemed cold and empty. She had enjoyed sharing a meal with someone. It was nice not to go into the house by herself and to have someone with whom she could discuss her passion for photography.

She sucked in a breath. Being around Taylor made her feel like a desirable, interesting woman. To everyone in town she was "Doc" first and foremost. Until Taylor had arrived, she'd had no idea she missed being thought of as a person. She had to stay alert, think sharply to keep up with him. It was invigorating on a number of levels to have Taylor around. Even if the man made her temper flare faster than anyone else could.

He'd hardly been there four days. She had no doubt that she would miss him when he left. And leave he would.

"Greg, what're you doing here again?" Shelby asked in bewilderment when she walked into the waiting room to call her next patient on Friday afternoon. "Surely he hasn't stuck something else up his nose?" she said, looking at the boy's mother for confirmation.

The mother shook her head slowly.

"His ear?" Shelby asked with a note of disbelief surrounding her words.

The mother gave a negative shake of her head. "The other doctor told us to come back."

"Dr. Stiles?"

"Yeah."

Shelby couldn't imagine why Taylor had asked Greg's mother to bring him in if there was no reason. Other than the propensity to always put things where they didn't belong, Greg was a healthy child, too healthy, in fact.

"I'll let Dr. Stiles know you're here." She didn't like the fact that patients were now coming in to see Taylor. They had always been her patients. He wasn't staying around long and she didn't want the community to start relying on him. She didn't want to start to count on him.

Shelby went to her office where she'd left Taylor minutes earlier completing some paperwork. They'd taken to rotating time behind the desk to get their charting completed. Taylor opened the office door as she prepared to enter and she walked right into him.

"Whoa." His hand circled her waist and pulled her against him to stop her from falling.

A larger-than-average guy, he seemed even more overpowering close up. With her nose pressed against him, she smelled like soap and a unique scent. It surrounded her, drawing her to him.

A low rumble filled his chest. "If you're not careful you're going to fall at my feet."

Putting her hands on his chest, she pushed away. His chuckle reminded her she was still in his arms. "If you'd let me go, I could stand."

He did, and she rocked back and gained her footing, unsure if she was off balance because he'd been holding her or because he'd let her go so quickly.

"Were you looking for me?" he asked, as if he thought she'd been on a personal quest.

"I was, but only because you have a patient. Greg, the boy whose nose you removed the bean from, is here. His mother said they were to see you. Did you tell them to come in for a follow-up exam?"

"I did ask them to stop by."

"Why?"

"Come with me and you'll see." He allowed her to walk ahead of him up the hall.

If she'd had patients waiting she would've argued that she didn't have time for show and tell but for once the waiting room was empty, something that happen more often now that Taylor was helping out.

Even the time she spent working at home had gotten shorter. Taylor had been in town less than a week and he was already having a big impact on her life. He was efficient and thorough, and some of the patients were starting to warm up to him. When they came into the waiting room, Greg popped down from his mother's lap and ran to Taylor. "I good. Sucker." Greg tugged on Taylor's well-pressed slacks.

Taylor pulled something out of his pocket before squatting down on one heel, which brought him close to eye level with the boy.

Holding out a sucker, Taylor said, "Greg, you were good. You didn't stick anything in your nose for a week. Now, if you want another one you have to be good for two weeks. I won't be here but I'm sure Doc Wayne will give you one." Taylor looked at her for confirmation.

Something about Taylor not being there when the boy came back caused a catch in her chest. Pushing the thought to a back drawer in her mind, Shelby nodded and said to Greg, "I'll have it waiting for you. But you can't put anything in your nose or ears."

The boy nodded, unwrapped the sucker and popped it into his mouth, his cheeks going chubby with his wide smile.

The mother nodded her thanks, took the boy's hand and headed for the door. With them gone, Shelby turned to Taylor. "How did you know?"

"As soon as I removed the bean he started begging for a sucker. I asked his mother if you gave him one every time you removed something. She said yes and I knew something was up.

"Greg was stuffing his nose full in order to come here and get a sucker. I made a deal with him that if he didn't do it again then I'd see that he got one. I know how bad they are for the teeth but one thing at a time. You can wean him off them."

"It was a nice call. I should've caught on."

"Don't beat yourself up. You can't do it all perfectly. You have a lot to see about here. Greg's fine and now you know. Just keep weaning him off. Soon it won't be a problem. Let up on yourself."

"I still should have realized what he was doing. Thanks."

"You don't have to sound like you're in pain when you say that."

She gave him a wry smile. "It's a little excruciating to admit I missed something so simple."

"You'll get it next time," he said, going to the reception desk.

Later that evening at closing time, Taylor said, "Hey, Mr. Teems gave me coupons for a free ice cream down at the Cream Castle. Why don't we all go and get a banana split after we close?"

"I've got a date. Got to go," Carly said, picking up her purse.

He turned to Shelby.

"I don't think so."

"Oh, come on, Shelby. Do something a little spontaneous for a change. All that paperwork will be here when you get back. I'll even help you."

"I still don't think so. And I don't need your help with my paperwork."

"Look, have pity on a stranger in town. I'm not even sure how to get there. I told Mr. Teems I'd stop by."

"Still—"

"I know you missed lunch because I did. Let's make this our supper."

"Well, put like that…"

"Great. I'll drive."

Even though she'd been hard to convince, it didn't take her long to get her purse, lock up and climb into his car.

"Which way?" He backed out of what had become his usual parking space.

"The best way to go is out to the bypass. Turn left out of the parking lot." She leaned her head back and closed her eyes.

She had to be worn out. He was. "Bypass? This town isn't large enough to have a bypass."

"They built it when the talk started about building a lake."

"Lake?"

"Lake Benton. The hope is that it'll bring business to this area. It'll be another couple of years, though, before there's water."

"From what little I've seen of the area, it could use it." He glanced her way. Her hair blew around her face. She looked totally relaxed. Something he'd rarely seen.

"It can. Most of the young people are leaving because there're no jobs. Make a left at the next light," she said, just loud enough that he could hear her over the wind. For the first time she'd not growled when he'd said something negative about the town, a sure sign she was tired.

"The Cream Castle is a mile down on the right." She indicated after he'd driven another mile.

He pulled into the gravel parking lot. They got out and walked to the window of the white building with the bright red awning. "One vanilla ice cream cone and one banana split with the works," he told the teenager at the window. "I used to work in a place like this when I was in high school."

"Really? I would've thought from looking at you that you would've spent all your time on the football or baseball field, being a star."

"Couldn't stay out of trouble long enough," he said flatly.

His words held a bitterness that surprised Shelby. The skinny teen with the earring pushed Taylor's huge banana split toward him and handed her the cone, stopping further questions.

Taylor took a seat on the bench of the cement table next to the building. He must have seen her hesitate and look towards the car because he said in a voice that wouldn't consent to an argument, "No way are we carrying this in my car. You can take a few minutes to enjoy." He dug a spoon into the bowl of nuts and chocolate sauce. "Mmm. Good," he said as he pulled the plastic spoon from his mouth.

"So you've found something in this town you like," Shelby said as she sat down and gave her ice cream a long lick.

Taylor's gaze lifted to meet hers. "I've found a few things."

If she wasn't careful, the ice cream in her hand would melt all over her fingers from the heat surging through her. Just as quickly his concentration returned to his ice cream. Was she reading something into what he'd said? Imagining things? Nothing was going to happen between them. He was just flirting. "What's Mr. Lambert's story?"

Shelby blinked. His question out of the blue caught her by surprise. The eighty-year-old man had refused to see Taylor earlier in the day, insisting that Shelby was the only one he would allow to take care of him.

"Some of the people around here are very set in their ways. He's lived in the same hollow a few miles out of town his entire life. He's tough. Been a logger since he was a boy. You wouldn't believe the house he lives in. No indoor plumbing. Animals living inside in the winter." Shelby shuddered. "It took me almost a year before Mr. Lambert would let me see him. It wasn't until he hurt his hand and his daughter came to get me that I ever took care of him."

"You do house calls?"

"When I have to. You know, it may be hard for some of the patients to relate to you because your clothes and shoes cost enough to feed their entire family for a year."

"There's nothing wrong with liking nice things."

"No, there isn't. Don't get me wrong, you look great—"

"Why, thank you, Shelby."

"That's not what I meant. I just think some of the older patients might find you less, uh, intimidating if you maybe wore jeans and tennis shoes."

"Would you find me less intimidating?" His look bored into hers.

Somehow this conversation had gotten off track. "You don't intimidate me," Shelby said with as much conviction as she could muster.

His spoon fell into the empty plastic tray with

a clunk, and he leaned back as if in deep thought. "I'm not sure you're telling me the truth, but that's beside the point. I also think it might surprise you just how much I know about how people around here think."

"Really?"

"Yes, but we need to be getting back. I promised to help you out with that charting."

"That's okay, I can manage it."

"I know you can. But I'm going to help anyway."

Shelby rubbed her hand along the seat of Taylor's car as they rode down the road a few minutes later. "You know, this is a nice car."

"Now, that wasn't that hard to admit, was it?"

She laughed, "No I guess it wasn't. I do love riding with the top down."

The sound of a police siren pierced the air.

Taylor's sharp word made her wince. He slowly pulled off onto the shoulder of the road and turned off the engine. His jaw muscles jumped and his hand shook almost imperceptibly as he leaned across her to reach into the glove compartment. She wouldn't have noticed if he hadn't been so close. "I'll handle this," he said gruffly.

"I know I wasn't speeding," he said, more to himself than to her.

The deputy hadn't even approached the car yet and Taylor was angry. It seemed over the top. "Maybe you just have a taillight out?" Shelby suggested.

He glared at her. His look prevented her from offering further comments. "No hick deputy's going to give me a ticket for doing nothing," he mumbled as he pulled his wallet from his hip pocket and dug for his license.

"Hey, Shelby, I thought that was you," the deputy said from where he stood beside Taylor's door.

"Hi, Sam." Shelby smiled up at the man.

Taylor gave her an odd look before switching his attention to the deputy. Holding out his license and insurance information, Taylor looked even more exasperated when the deputy didn't immediately take them.

"I don't need those. I just wanted to see if Shelby's planning to bring her famous carrot cake to the block party."

A look of confusion then disbelief washed over Taylor's face. Shelby had to work to keep a straight face. "I hadn't planned to but since you asked I'll be sure to bake one. By the way, this is Dr. Stiles. He's working with me for a couple of weeks."

Sam looked down at Taylor. "Nice to meet you, Doc." His attention didn't linger but returned to Shelby. "I do love your carrot cake."

"Sam, that's so sweet."

Taylor's facial expression turned to complete disgust. Her grin grew. *And he thought he understood small towns.*

"We have to go. Sam. See you Saturday."

The palm of Sam's hand double-thumped the top of the car door. "I look forward to it."

Taylor started the car and pulled out onto the road. She had the impression he wished he could spin gravel and roar off, but instead he moved into traffic as if he was learning to drive.

"Just what was that all about?" he asked, his voice full of wonder and irritation.

"You heard. Cake and the block party."

"Do the cops around here regularly pull people over to discuss a party?" He gave her an incredulous look.

Shelby shrugged. "I guess when they want to. What's the big deal?" He shook his head as if trying to make sense of an abstract painting. She leaned forward enough to see his face. "You really were afraid that you were being stopped for speeding." She made no effort to hide her amazement.

His eyes remained on the road and he didn't answer.

She continued to watch his face. Her eyes narrowed. "What aren't you telling me?"

He glanced at her. "I've had a few speeding tickets."

"How many is a few?"

"Enough that your uncle sent me here instead of to jail."

She gave a low whistle and grinned. "So-o-o, that's what Uncle Gene meant when he said, and I quote, 'He needs to slow down for a while.'" She giggled.

"It's not funny, Shelby."

She giggled again. "Oh, yes, it is. So this fancy car is a police magnet."

"Sometimes I was on the way to an emergency," he said indignantly.

"Really?" She drew the word out.

"There might've been a few times when I exaggerated a bit. Someone checked, and dear sweet

Uncle Gene decided to throw the book at me." His top lip curled as he said the last few words.

Shelby slapped her leg and howled with laughter. "So your lead foot got you sent to me." She gave his shoulder a friendly shove. "Uncle Gene has always been creative in his rulings."

"He outdid himself this time," Taylor grumbled.

For some reason, Taylor's obvious agitation tickled Shelby's funny bone. "What're you? Sixteen?"

Taylor pulled the car into his parking space next to her truck. "Now you're really making fun of me."

She laughed. "I'm sorry." Tears filled her eyes.

"Doesn't sound like it."

Shelby couldn't stop the merriment that continued to roll up from deep within her belly. She'd not laughed like this in years.

"It's not that funny," Taylor said, turning to look at her.

"I'm trying to stop but I can't help thinking about your face when you found out you'd been stopped because of a cake." Her laughter bubbled over again.

"Okay, that is kind of funny." His chuckle intertwined with her giggles. "Now I think you've had enough fun at my expense. If you don't stop…"

"What're you going to do?" She pointed at him. "You should have seen your face."

Another peal of mirth escaped her.

"Okay, that did it." Before she realized his intent, he'd grabbed her by the top of her arms and pulled her towards him. His mouth came down to cover hers.

Her laughter caught in her throat. His lips were firm, warm and confident. A red-hot flow of desire went through her. She didn't move. His mouth shifted to the side, finding a more secure place, sealing her mouth completely with his. For moments of pure bliss her world was nothing but Taylor's kiss. He pulled away and her eyelids fluttered open seconds after his hands no longer held her.

"I told you to stop."

She stared at his lips. "You did." Even to her own ears she sounded wistful. "I'll try to remember not to laugh at you again."

"That would be a good idea, unless you want more of the same."

"I don't." With effort she made the words sound sharp in the hope that it covered her true reaction. She couldn't make more of the kiss than it was. He was just trying to stop her from laughing at him, that was all.

"We'll see about that, but for now I think we should go in and get started on that paperwork." He stepped out of the car and Shelby followed more slowly.

She loved her husband. Missed him, but she'd never felt the fire with him that she'd experienced during Taylor's kiss. A shiver skated through her. If she had that kind of reaction to one playful kiss from Taylor, what would it be like to be on the receiving end of one of his seductive ones?

It was Saturday afternoon and Taylor's foot lay heavily on the gas pedal of the car. He was driving too fast but he couldn't get past the thought of what he had done yesterday evening.

God, he'd kissed Shelby and he desperately wanted to do it again. What had he been thinking? That was the problem, he hadn't been thinking. He'd reacted. The kiss had been far too short, far too cautious. He wanted to experience Shelby meeting him kiss for kiss, explore her wonderfully sensual mouth. He'd been hurt as a kid by laughter and ridicule but hers had made him want to join her. When he'd been a middle-school student, laughter at his expense had been an everyday occurrence. With her, he found he could appreciate the humor also.

But to kiss her. It only complicated things.

That he didn't need or want. He didn't even know how to give what Shelby would surely demand. He'd never been on the inside of a functional relationship. His parents' marriage certainly hadn't been a sterling example.

Shaking his head and lifting his foot a little, he slowed the car. As always Shelby had been efficient and businesslike at the clinic that morning but there had been a change towards him. He should've been glad she wanted to remain at arm's length but he didn't like the idea one bit and he wasn't sure why.

It'd been a relief to say, "I'm out of here. See you Monday morning."

Shelby had nodded her understanding without looking up from the chart she was studying. Her giving him the cold shoulder irritated him.

What she thought of him or, for that matter, what the other hick people in this nothing town thought didn't matter. He had one more week to serve and he'd be out of there, never to think of any of them again. Right now he was getting some time away from Benton and Shelby and he planned to make the most of it.

The outskirts of Nashville were coming up quickly when his cellphone rang. It was his date for the evening, telling him she wasn't going to make the opera after all.

Taylor continued his conversation as he watched a state patrolman turn around and get behind him. The speedometer on the sports car let him know that he wasn't over the limit. At the next exit Taylor pulled off the interstate. With relief, he watched the patrol car go on down the road. All he needed was to be caught in town speeding. That would really make "Uncle Gene" irate. With no one expecting him now, he decided to play it safe and head back to Benton. He didn't need to take a chance on being sentenced to more time at the clinic.

Would it really be that bad to be stuck in Benton longer? With Shelby?

CHAPTER FOUR

SHELBY loved the quarterly block parties. She had little time to socialize and she made a point of joining these. They were an opportunity to connect with neighbors and one of the best parts of living in a small town.

She adored living in Benton and didn't understand Taylor's aversion to the town. Carly thought he was the best thing to come along since texting. To her surprise, she herself had nothing to complain about where his professional skills were concerned but she shouldn't learn to rely on him as he wasn't going to stay. It was a shame because the next doctor might not relate to her patients as well as Taylor did.

Some of the people had been slow to warm up to him but that was changing. If she did have an issue, it was that she had this unexplained attraction to him that made her feel uneasy. But the feeling of comfort and contentment at being surrounded by people who cared about you and watched after you washed over her, easing away her troubles.

Shelby swished her hips more than necessary as she carried her plate loaded with food to the folding chair she'd brought from home. The occasion not only let her leave the clinic problems for a while but gave her a chance to wear one of the sundresses she had hanging in her closet. The lightweight fabric with the tiny rosebuds brushed against her skin, making her feel very feminine. Something she hadn't experienced in a long time. At least, not until Taylor had come rolling into town.

He'd managed to make her feel warm, soft and womanly more than once, but she shook her head. She had no business thinking that way about him or his kiss. He was off with another woman. Taylor had no real interest in *her*. She was just the doctor he had to put up with until he'd done his time and could go home.

She sat with her neighbors in a lawn chair under a large oak tree to eat her meal and listened to their chatter. The saying "lonely in a crowd" flitted through her mind. Nibbling at her food, she placed the half-eaten meal on the ground. Leaning her head back against the top of the chair, she closed her eyes and enjoyed the warmth of the sun on her face. And drifted off.

A rustling noise nearby woke her. She lifted her eyelids, rolled her head in the direction of the sound and straightened in the chair. "What're you doing here? I thought you were in Nashville."

Taylor grinned. "And hello to you too." He took a seat in the empty chair next to her.

He looked completely at home in khaki shorts, knit shirt and leather sandals but his demeanor still screamed cosmopolitan man. Among her neighbors Taylor stood out but she had no doubt he would in any crowd. He was the type of man who drew attention and admiration.

A tingle flitted through her. She was happy to see him. Maybe too happy. "Why're you here, Taylor?"

"Mmm. Plans changed." He took a bite out of a fried chicken leg.

She lowered her voice. "I didn't think this was your idea of a good time. Too small town."

"It's not. I was pulling into the drive and Mr. Carter flagged me down. Said you were down here. He insisted I come too. I gave in." His shoulders rose and fell. "Heck, I've got nothing better to do." He bit into the chicken again.

"Please don't hurt their feelings."

"Are you implying I don't know how to behave?" His skin drew taut across his strong jaw. Had she made him angry?

"You've made it clear on more than one occasion that you think you're too good for Benton," she whispered.

"I might not want to stay here for ever, but I do know how to be sociable and gracious when I have the right incentive."

"Incentive?"

His eyes bored into hers and then dropped to her lips. A flash of heat sped through her. Warmth pooled low in her belly. She wrapped her arms around her waist. Was he trying to coerce her into another kiss? Or more?

"Yeah, I wanted to see if the cake that the cop with the crush on you likes so much is that good." At the whoosh of her breath, he grinned. "Did you have something else in mind?"

"I did not. The cake's inside. Help yourself." She pointed in the direction of the door into the house from the carport.

Taylor stood and offered his hand to her. "Why don't you show me?"

Mrs. Nettleboom, the elderly lady who lived

across the street, walked up. "Well, Dr. Stiles, I see you found her."

"Yes, I did. Thank you for pointing me in the correct direction. I was just telling Shelby how much I'd enjoy having some of that cake I've been hearing about." The woman nearly preened under the grin Taylor gave her. "The deputy over there..." he nodded in the direction of a group of men "...thought it was good enough to pull us over to ask about."

"That sounds like little Sam. He loves Shelby's carrot cake," Mrs. Nettleboom cooed. "He always requests that she bring it. Always makes sure he cuts an extra piece to take to the station the next day."

Taylor looked at Shelby and smirked. "He does, does he?"

"Honey," the woman said to Shelby, "go on and take this nice young man in and get him a slice."

Shelby feared she was well on her way to having a sugar stroke from listening to their conversation. The only way to put an end to it was to do as Mrs. Nettleboom instructed.

Ignoring his offer to help, she picked up her plate and stood. He trailed close behind her as she walked up the drive. She dropped her plate into the garbage beside the door and entered the house. "The desserts are in the kitchen."

The counter space was covered with cakes, pies and sweets of all kinds. Shelby waved her hand. "Help yourself. The plates and plastic forks are on the table," Shelby said.

The cozy kitchen suddenly didn't feel large enough for both of them. Taylor's presence filled the area, pressing against her. She needed to leave.

His hand gently circled her forearm, making her start. "Which one is yours?" he asked, much too close.

Shelby paused. His fingers slipped along her skin and away. "It's the cake on the blue plate over there." The touch had been casual but there was nothing ordinary about her body's reaction.

"You're not going to have any?"

"Not right now. Maybe later." She circled past the kitchen counter and headed out the door, grateful for the breeze that blew outside.

Had the kiss made her skittish? Taylor couldn't imagine strong, willful Shelby being intimidated by him or anyone else. She apparently didn't even trust him long enough to stay in the same room with him. He didn't like that at all. Taking the kiss back wasn't possible, even if he wanted to and he didn't. Instead he could only think of kissing her again but this time like she deserved to be kissed. Long, sweet and deep.

He ran his fingers through his hair. The last few days they'd worked together had been nice. The cases had been interesting and he found he liked working beside someone who so obviously cared about her patients and their feelings. Something he'd not always experienced in a large hospital.

He'd messed up with that kiss and he didn't know how to fix it.

Taylor cut a large slice of Shelby's cake, put it on a plate and carried it outside. Shelby wasn't visible anywhere. As he headed toward his chair the old insecure feeling of not being accepted made his stomach clench. He gained control by reminding himself that he was no longer the kid of the town drunk. No one here knew his secret. Instead he was a doctor and a well-respected one.

Still, he was surprised when Mr. Carter called, "Hey, Doc, come have a seat with us." Squaring his shoulders, he said, "Sure," with more enthusiasm than he felt and took the open place at the table.

Taylor filled his fork with cake and put it in

his mouth. Taking a moment to savor the sweetness, he said, "You're right. It's great." He lifted his utensil in the direction of Shelby's boyfriend cop, who was seated across from him.

"Yeah, Shelby has many talents," the deputy said, grinning at Taylor.

"Don't mind him," Mr. Carter said, nudging the younger man in the ribs. "He's had a crush on her for ages, but she won't even look his way."

Lightness replaced the twinge of possessiveness in Taylor's heart. That baffled him. He and Shelby didn't have that kind of relationship. Their relationship didn't warrant jealousy. Yet, as illogical as it was, the pang had still been there.

Mr. Roster, a thin, white-headed man, said, "We're glad you're here to help out our Shelby. She works too hard. I know she has appreciated having you around."

Taylor wasn't so sure about that. "I'm only going to be at the clinic for another week then I'm headed home."

"You're not staying?" a man from the other end of the table asked. "We thought you might decide to make it permanent."

"No, this was only a temporary assignment." Taylor slid the last bit of cake off his fork, wishing he had more. Shelby certainly had other abilities besides caring for people and photography.

The conversation changed to the construction of the new dam that would create a recreational lake and what the town might expect from the influx of people. As for whether or not there would be a big change, the jury seemed to be out. Taylor listened, offering little input. The lake wasn't his worry. He'd be long gone.

When there was a lull in the conversation he looked around and asked, "Where did Shelby go?"

"I saw her heading around the side of the house. She had her camera," Mr. Roster said, before returning to the conversation with the others.

Minutes later, Taylor excused himself and strolled in the direction Shelby had gone. Children's laughter and the soft tinkle of Shelby's amusement told him he'd headed in the correct direction. Going through the gate of the chain-link fence, he found Shelby snapping pictures of a young girl as she glided back and forth on a swing set. A group of middle-school boys played baseball nearby.

Taylor leaned against a tree and watched. Encouraging the girl to continue swinging, Shelby moved around, taking pictures from different angles. Her dress blew around her legs in the light breeze, accenting her shapely behind. Occasionally, Shelby gave the thin strap of her dress an impatient push up her slim shoulder from where it had slipped. Taylor smiled. He liked seeing her relaxed, the worry lines on her face gone. She deserved an easier life but he wasn't the one to give her that.

The entire scene looked like a Norman Rockwell painting. Taylor had never really identified with images of Rockwell's homespun family life, because his own childhood had never been anything near resembling the pictures. Shelby brought that hometown feeling to life right in front of his eyes. He bet her photos would turn out to be wonderful. Unfortunately, she became so uptight around him he doubted he'd ever be invited to see them.

"You're dumb."

"Yeah, nobody likes you."

The ugly words took a moment to work their way through Shelby's concentration on the picture's subject.

"Everyone hates you."

Taking the viewfinder away from her eye, she

turned to where the boys crowded around the smallest boy.

Before she could intervene, Taylor stalked past her. She'd been so absorbed in finding the right shot she'd not realized he stood nearby. He went to stand behind the child the others faced and placed his hand on the boy's shoulder.

"Now, what's going on here?" Taylor's gaze fell on each individual long enough so that they each looked at their feet instead of at Taylor. "Well?" he demanded in an even voice but giving the word a sharp edge.

A boy's head rose. "He always messes up. He doesn't know how to play."

"I see. And you do everything you try right all the time?"

The boy rubbed his bare foot back and forth in the dirt. "No, but—"

"Exactly. So why don't you let me and...?" He looked down at the boy in front of him.

"Charlie," the boy murmured.

"So why don't you let Charlie and I be a team and play against you guys?"

"That wouldn't be fair," a heavyset boy in the group complained. "You're big."

"No more than it's fair when three people gang

up on one. How do you think you would feel? So why don't you guys try to play something that Charlie might be good at?"

Taylor looked at Charlie again.

"I'm pretty good at basketball," he said in a stronger voice than he'd used earlier.

"Great," Taylor said. "I saw a hoop in the drive-way next door. Why don't you guys head that way?"

"I don't really like basketball," the leader of the group said.

"Why's that?" Taylor asked.

"Because he ain't any good at it," a tall, thin boy offered.

Taylor said nothing but look pointedly at the leader.

"Come on, guys. Let's go find a ball," the boy finally offered.

Shelby watched in amazement as the group walked past her on their way out the gate.

"Lauren, honey," she told the girl she'd been taking pictures of, "I bet your mother's looking for you. It's getting late."

The girl ran behind the boys towards the front of the house.

Taylor stood rigid, staring off into the distance.

His breaths were coming shallow and fast as if he fought a demon. What was going on?

"Taylor?"

She received no response.

"Taylor?"

As if coming out of a trance, he looked at her but without really seeing her.

"You okay?"

"Oh, yeah, sure." A look of recognition flickered in his eyes.

"What you did with those boys was impressive. Did you get a child psych degree along with that MD?"

Taylor visibly relaxed, regaining his causal manner. "Nothing to it."

He might say that but she knew better.

The green light of fireflies blinked around them as they walked back along the sidewalk toward her house.

"Was the block party as bad as you thought it would be?" Shelby asked.

Taylor gave her a sideways glance. "I never said it was going to be bad."

"You sure acted that way."

He stuffed his hands in the pockets of his shorts. "It wasn't exactly what I'd expected."

"How's that?"

"I didn't think your neighbors would be so accepting of me. It has been my experience that small towns are pretty close knit. Don't let people in who don't fit their idea of acceptable. Shall we say judgmental?"

"Really?" she remarked, enjoying the soft breeze and the ruffling of Taylor's shirt against his body. "I grew up in a small town and I thought we were a wonderfully supportive group of people."

"Apparently you lived on the right side of the tracks." The words had a raw-edged roughness to them.

She searched his face. "What's that supposed to mean?"

He glanced at her. "That not everyone has such great memories of living in a small town."

"Why don't you just come on out with it? Quit beating around the bush."

He looked around the street as if he was searching for something. The words, the right way to say them or the answer? She wasn't sure which.

Her fingertips touched his forearm briefly. He was warm, firm and all male.

"We aren't that different in some ways." He stated his words slowly. "I grew up in a town much like this one but in Kentucky."

"Really? I never would have guessed."

"And I had no intention that you ever would. It isn't something I share."

"Why not?" She didn't try to keep her astonishment out of her voice.

"I've worked hard to put that time, that place behind me." He stopped short, turned and looked at her.

"What happened?" she asked quietly.

His eyes turned stone hard then he stalked ahead. Shelby jogged to catch up, her sandals making a slapping noise against the concrete and her camera bouncing against her side from where the strap hung over her shoulder. When she came alongside him he began talking but didn't slow his pace.

"If you must know, I'm the son of the town drunk and the kid who used his fists to prove his worth." He snapped the words like gunshots.

Shelby slowed, stopped and watched as Taylor stalked off. It didn't surprise her that Taylor hadn't noticed she was no longer panting beside him. He'd slipped into his past.

By the time she'd reached her back door, he'd entered the apartment and effectively shut the world and her out.

At mid-morning on Sunday Shelby sat at her kitchen table, paying her personal bills as well as the clinic's. A knock at the door interrupted her concentration. Before she could move, the door opened and Taylor's head appeared.

"Taylor!" Shelby let out a squeak and pulled her lightweight robe over her thin gown. "You can't just barge into my house uninvited. I'm not even dressed."

"I knocked." His look traveled to her bare toes and slowly upwards until his gaze met hers. There was a twinkle of appreciation in his coffee-colored eyes. "Nice outfit."

Heat zipped to her cheeks. He had a way of making her blush and she was entirely too old for such silliness. "What do you need? I'm trying to get some work done."

"You know, it would be nice for you to be happy to see me just once."

She was glad to see that his bad mood from the day before had disappeared. She huffed.

He grinned. "How about showing me around? Maybe take me out to where they're building the dam for the lake?"

"I don't know. I've tons of paperwork to do." She waved her hand toward the table where the bills were stacked. "There might be an emergency and I'll be needed."

"And there might not be. You work too hard. It's not healthy. You need some down time to be ready for your patients. Besides, you'll have your cellphone with you."

Why this sudden interest in Benton, and the lake? She'd been surprised to see his car still parked in the drive this morning after the way they'd parted the evening before. She'd expected him to spend his day off far away from Benton. But she didn't plan to ruin his cheerful mood by quizzing him about his past now. "Okay, I guess this can wait."

"Get dressed. I'll wait." Taylor pulled a chair out from under the table, sat and propped an ankle over his knee.

He looked at home in her house and that disturbed her. He'd only been there a week and already he seemed like he belonged. It had been too easy to get used to having him around. When he left, which he'd assured her he would, she'd be on her own again. If she let him into her life there would be heartache and that she wouldn't chance.

Given little choice and beginning to look forward to spending time away from her mundane responsibilities, she headed to her bedroom to change. It would be nice to spend a day having fun, something she didn't often do.

She returned dressed similarly to Taylor in cutoff jeans, a T-shirt and sandals. He looked less like the slick, fashion-plate doctor and more like a regular guy out looking for adventure. She liked this newer version. This one she understood better. He smiled at her and her hand trembled as she pushed a stray strand of hair behind her ear.

"Come on," Taylor said impatiently. "Don't forget your camera," he said over his shoulder as the door slapped into place.

"Stop telling me what to do," she called after him in a playful voice, even though she was grateful for the reminder. She hadn't thought of taking her camera. At one time it had been as attached to her as her skin, though life and the clinic had pushed photography way down on her priority list. With a sudden feeling of liberation she picked up her case and followed him outside.

He opened his car door.

"Hey," she called, "if you want to really see the area, we need to go in my truck. The bottom of that car might not survive the back roads."

He gave the small battered truck a dubious look but slammed his car door shut. "Is there enough room for my legs in that thing?"

"You'll be fine."

Shelby slipped behind the wheel and couldn't help but grin as she watched Taylor settle in beside her. He overwhelmed the small interior. And her too. For once, she wished she drove a larger vehicle.

As she shifted into reverse, the back of her hand slid across his bare knee. The gears made a grinding sound as she found the correct slot. She glanced at Taylor. His mouth lifted slightly at the corners. She took special care that her fingers remained on the top of the gearshift instead of gripping it with her hand in order to avoid touching Taylor's knee again. She put the truck into first gear.

Pulling out onto the highway, she said, "I'm surprised you're interested in sightseeing."

"Not so much interested as bored. There's not even a movie theater in this town."

"We have some culture." She refused to become defensive.

"How's that? The cultures at the clinic?"

"Funny. No, we have a museum."

"What kind?"

She grinned. "The Benton Historical Museum."

"Figures."

His low chuckle rippled through her like water over stones in a brook. She wanted to hear that sound again. He'd relaxed somewhat since he'd arrived in town. Even the lines around his eyes had become less noticeable.

Shelby slowed for the car in front of them to make a turn. She looked at him. "You know," she said causally but with meaning, "for someone who insisted I show them around, you're not being very nice."

He gave her a lopsided grin. "I'm sorry. I'll keep my snide remarks to myself. So why did you and your husband decide Benton was the place to start a clinic?"

"Because this county qualified for state assistance and we thought it would be a great place to raise children."

Shelby winced. After his admission yesterday, he wouldn't be impressed by that plan. Thankfully the road she'd been looking for came into sight. She made a left turn.

"Where're we headed?"

"I thought you wanted to see the lake. Also there's a spot along here where I'd like to get some pictures. The last time I made it out this way the light wasn't right. Today it looks perfect. I won't be long."

"I've got nothing but time." He ran one tan arm along the back of the seat, his fingers falling inches above her shoulder.

When she changed gears, the tips of his fingers brushed the top of her shoulder. Supersensitive to each touch, she was thankful when she found the place where she could ease off onto the grassy roadside. "There's an old house in the woods here. I'll snap a few pictures and be right back."

"I'll come with you."

"It's pretty rough walking."

"Please, don't insult my manhood," he said in disgust as he opened the door and climbed out.

Shelby followed suit, finding the path that hunters or animals used and following it into the stand of pines.

"I had no intention of besmirching your manhood." She certainly couldn't find anything to complain about in that department.

"Besmirching?" he said with interest. "I couldn't tell you the last time I heard that word used."

She glanced back at him. "Just because I live in a small town doesn't mean I don't know how to use big words."

"I was besmirched my entire childhood. Somehow using that word doesn't make it sound so bad."

She gave him a look of understanding and walked on. Taylor stayed close behind. She glanced back and found him sure-footed and confident as he walked over the pine-needle-padded track. He'd obviously done this type of hiking before.

"This area used to have head-high gullies. We'd play in them as kids. We'd show up at my dad's truck red from head to toe, covered in dirt."

"What caused the gullies?"

"Erosion of the farmland during the thirties and

forties. *Grapes of Wrath* type stuff. A forester who knew what he was doing bought up the land for almost nothing and planted pines. Now you can hardly tell there was ever a dip in the land."

"What's he doing with the land now?"

"When the trees mature they'll be harvested and turned into pulp for paper and the land re-planted. You know the renewable resource—trees."

"Yeah, I remember that old slogan. Just never saw it in action before."

Taylor was much more interested in watching the sway of Shelby's hips than hearing an environmental report. However, the more she talked the longer he had to enjoy the enticing view.

They'd not gone far before entering an open area. In the middle of a knoll stood a tumbledown shack built from clapboard that had mellowed to a pale gray. The porch, which extended across the entire front, listed on the right corner. A large oak tree stood off to the side, its limbs offering shade to half the house. Wildflowers grew in the knee-high grass surrounding the area.

It looked much like the house where he'd grown up, sharing a cramped bedroom with his two brothers. He refused to revisit those morose memories. The day was too pretty and he had too lovely a woman with him to let ugly thoughts spoil it. Last night had been difficult enough. He wouldn't let his emotions show like that again.

Shelby moved around, leaning one way and another then squatting as she brought the camera to her eye. He had no idea why she was so interested in taking pictures of the sad reminder of what had been. He spent every minute of his life trying to forget a place like this one.

When Shelby stepped onto the porch he headed towards her. "I don't think that's a good idea." His overprotective reaction surprised him. He usually let people do as they pleased. Fear that Shelby might get hurt disturbed him on a level he didn't wish to explore.

"I'm just going to stand here." She brought the camera to her face again. "I do know what I'm doing."

"Never doubted it," Taylor said, and went to lean a hand against the one post of the porch that appeared stable.

Taylor found he enjoyed discovering each new facet of Shelby's personality. She continued to surprise him daily. That aspect of being forced to be in Benton had turned into an interesting pastime. He tested the porch post for sturdiness then leaned his shoulder against it as he continued to watch her.

Standing, she stepped back a few feet. He straightened and she said, "No, don't move. I need to get a contrast in these. Something living and breathing."

With her camera still up to her eye, she continued to step back. He settled against the post again.

"That's great."

Click, click.

Shelby was totally engaged. She treated taking pictures just as she did working at the clinic. With complete absorption and focus. What would it be like to be on the receiving end of that focus? Was she just as intent and conscious of detail when making love?

Ooh, that wasn't a thought he should be having. Their plans for their lives diverged, not converged. She was the perfect house, perfect yard, and perfect family kind of person. He had no concept of that kind of life. It was like a fairy tale to him. He shifted, looking in the direction of a noise coming from under the trees.

"Stop right there," she ordered.

"What's wrong?"

"Nothing. It looks great."

Minutes later she breathed a sigh of satisfaction, suggesting she'd gotten all she wanted. Again he was thinking of things he had no business contemplating.

"I'm ready if you are."

Mind out of the bedroom, Stiles!

They made their way back to the truck. Just as they were preparing to cross the ditch bordering the road a yelping sound came from the weeds.

Shelby moved toward the sound, bent down and straightened out her hand. A tiny, deathly thin dog with matted hair sniffed at her fingers. "I hate it when people just throw animals out. I can't imagine what kind of person does that."

My father.

Shelby picked up the dog.

"What do you plan to do with him?" Taylor asked.

She turned to him as if he was suggesting they commit murder. "We can't leave it here!"

"I wasn't suggesting that we do. I was just wondering what you were thinking. Keeping him?"

"I'll just take him home and clean him up. Then see if I can find a home for him."

"He looks like he might need to see a vet."

"I'll see about that tomorrow. There's an old blanket behind my seat in the truck—would you get it?"

Did she take home every stray animal she found? In many ways he was one, and she had taken him in. "Sure."

He returned with the blanket and handed it to her. She wrapped the panic-stricken animal in it, bringing the dog close to her chest. "It'll be all right, little one. I'll take care of you," she cooed. She said to Taylor, "We're almost at the lake. I'll show it to you and then we'll head home and take care of this cutie."

Cutie. There was nothing cute about the sad little animal. For a brief second Taylor was jealous of the puppy and the attention it was receiving.

"Would you mind?" She indicated that she'd like him to hold the dog.

Taylor reached out for the bundle. He looked down at the dog, and the mixed-breed mutt with one floppy ear and wiry hair looked at Taylor as if he was his savior.

"He seems to like you." Shelby smiled at Taylor.

He grunted a response. He'd always wanted a

dog as a boy. His father had said no more than once and the last time had been with the back of his hand. Taylor hadn't asked again. When he'd been in college and later working he hadn't had time for a dog so he'd never considered getting one. He ran a finger along the head of the confused little animal. Maybe it wasn't too late for him to make a change in his life and have a dog?

CHAPTER FIVE

SHELBY steered the truck along the windy tree-lined road until it sloped sharply downwards. Ahead lay a wide open area. It was level and clear of trees, with two unmaintained roads intersecting at the bottom.

"What do you think about the lake?" she asked.

"Where's the water?"

She smiled at Taylor's incredulous tone. "The dam's down the road a couple of miles. It'll take a few years to fill."

Shelby shifted into reverse.

"Hey! What're you doing? Aren't we going to drive across?"

"I don't think so. We're really not supposed to be this far down the road."

"Come on, Shelby. Live a little. I don't think the only doctors for miles around are going to be sent to jail for driving across a dry lake bed."

Taylor had managed to make her sound silly. With a huff of resignation Shelby changed gears.

She eased the truck into terrain that would soon be under water. They rocked and bumped over the uneven road where heavy equipment had crossed.

"You don't like driving through here, do you?" Taylor asked.

Had it been that obvious that it unnerved her? She needed to work on schooling her emotions or he'd learn things she'd rather keep hidden. Like her fear of caring too much for him, or her dread of being hurt. "There's something spooky about knowing that I should be under eight feet of water. I know it isn't rational but it makes me nervous. Maybe it's from watching old earthquake movies or something."

Taylor chuckled. "Interesting. So you're afraid of blood and dry lake beds."

She glanced at him. "What're you doing? Keeping a record?"

"I just find your little quirks intriguing." He grinned at her.

"Quirks? I don't have quirks."

"Okay. Foibles."

"Foibles! That makes me sound like I'm eighty."

A guffaw of Taylor's laughter filled the cab of

the truck. "You know, it's fun to tease you. You blush every time."

Taylor's smile only grew wider at her huff of dismissal. He enjoyed the pink color on her cheeks that wasn't disappearing. Had a woman ever been more desirable? Had he ever wanted to kiss one more? With great effort he kept his hands to himself. Slowly she eased the truck down into the lake bed. His smile grew.

They had reached an area where the narrow road intersected another. Shelby concentrated on downshifting, veering to the right faster than necessary but correcting before the truck went off the road. She was really spooked by being on the lake bed. The road sloped upwards as they traveled farther to what she thought of as dry land. Taylor delighted in the sight of Shelby's chest rising and falling with her sigh of relief.

"Glad to be back on shore?" he quipped.

She snarled, her upper lip in a mock look of displeasure. "Funny. Very funny."

Shelby was adorable. He couldn't remember spending a more enjoyable afternoon or one when he'd felt more sexually frustrated. The dog whimpered in his lap.

"We need to get him home. Feed him," she said, as much to herself as to Taylor.

We. It surprised him that her use of the word didn't disturb him. He kind of liked the sound of it. He'd been on his own so long that it was nice to be included, even if it had to do with a stray dog. Her kind of *we* he'd like to be a part of. If he knew how.

They were back out on the highway and headed towards town when Shelby pulled off in front of a small country store.

"I don't have anything around the house to feed him. I'll be right back." She climbed out of the truck.

A couple of grizzly looking men sat against the wall of the building, their wooden chairs leaning back on the back legs. From their appearance they could've been the same two guys who had hung out in front of the general store in Taylor's hometown. Men like these, he was sure, spent their days talking and spitting, and knew all the gossip in the county. Unfortunately, his family had provided much of the gossip back then.

The only time Taylor had ever seen one of those men move off the porch had been when he'd been around ten years old. A group of boys had followed Taylor into the store. When he'd caught them stealing they'd cornered him in the candy aisle and threatened to say that he was the thief. He had been preparing to fight when Old Man Carr, one of the men sitting out front, had stepped into the aisle and said, "Hey, you boys break it up."

The boys disappeared in seconds, leaving Taylor to stare up at Mr. Carr. "Sometimes it looks like life is ganging up on you," the old man said in a gravelly voice. "I hear you do good in school. If you use them smarts, you'll never have to worry about fighting boys like them again."

Those words had stuck with Taylor and he'd taken them to heart. He'd decided that he could make something of himself because of that old man. His had been the few encouraging words that an angry, rebellious boy had needed to hear. The ones that had dared him to dream, made him think his life could be more than battles and disillusionment.

Shelby came out of the store with a skip in her step and a smile on her face. That look would be something Taylor would definitely miss when he left.

Opening the door of the truck, she handed Taylor a small paper bag and climbed in.

"That stop sure made you happy." Taylor shifted the dog in his lap and put the bag on the floor between his feet.

"Yeah. I used to walk to an old general store much like this one. It always makes me feel good here."

"Same with me."

"You did?"

"Yeah, we even had the same type of old men hanging around out front."

She chuckled. "I think they just come with places like this."

Taylor glanced back at the men as Shelby pulled the truck onto the highway. Maybe so, but he wasn't sure that they all came with a Mr. Carr. No matter how hard Taylor worked at it as they wound their way back home, he couldn't seem to leave that part of his life behind.

Shelby stopped the truck in her drive and turned the engine off. She reached over to take the puppy.

"He's sleeping. I'll hold him until you get his food ready." He cradled the dog in the crook of his arm as he opened the passenger door. "You get the food." He kicked the truck door closed with his heel.

In the kitchen, Shelby emptied the can of puppy food she'd bought into a bowl. Taylor set the puppy down. He wandered around the floor on weak legs.

"Come here, sweetie," Shelby placed the bowl on the floor. The dog tentatively approached the food. "Good boy," she cooed.

"You know," Taylor whispered, "if you talked to me like that, I'd do whatever you asked."

Her head jerked up. She glared at him. "You're making fun of me again."

A few seconds went by with the only sound coming from the dog eating with gusto.

"Maybe a little bit. But I can't help myself. I love your reactions. Like now. If looks could kill…" He looked down at the dog. "You know, this ragamuffin isn't the only one who's hungry. Is the burger joint open on Sunday?"

"No."

"You got anything I could fix us a meal out of?"

"I think I have some hamburger meat in the fridge."

"Great." The look on her face said she'd not

planned to have dinner with him. He ignored it. "I'll cook while you see about the dog."

"You asking or telling?"

"More like suggesting."

"Only because I'm hungry too will I accept your suggestion. The frying pan is under there." She pointed to a lower cabinet then picked up the little dog with the now rounded belly. "I shouldn't be long."

Shelby returned with a wiggling puppy in her hands as she dried him off with a towel. Taylor stood at the stove, flipping burgers. There was something nice about having a man cook for her.

"How'd the bath go?" He turned in her direction when she entered. "Looks like you might've had one too." Taylor gaze didn't meet hers. Instead it was focused further south.

His eyes had darkened, grown intent. She'd not had someone look at her like that in a long time. Jim had loved her. She'd never doubted that, but he had never regarded her with the same intensity, the same longing that Taylor showed now.

A river of heat flowed swiftly and sweetly through her, making her heart do the two-step. She glanced down and found that a large wet spot covered her breasts. Spinning round, she covered her embarrassment as well as her reaction to his regard. With a couple of quick rubs, she set the puppy on the floor and returned to her bedroom.

"You don't have to change on my account," he called. "I was enjoying the view."

Closing the door to her bedroom with a firm click, she sat on the bed and put her hands over her hot cheeks. She'd blushed more since Taylor had ridden into town than she had in her whole life before that.

She re-entered the kitchen in a dry shirt, to find the table set and a platter of burgers and buns front and center. It was good to have the kitchen used to prepare a real meal. She didn't cook often, it wasn't for just one.

"Got any chips to go with these burgers?" he asked.

Obviously those few heated moments earlier hadn't affected Taylor but they'd set her well-ordered world spinning.

"In the refrigerator freezer."

"The freezer?" he asked incredulously.

"Keeps them fresh. I'm not around enough and the chips go stale."

She sat in her usual chair while Taylor found the chips.

"You work too hard." The bag rattled as he opened it and stuck his hand in.

"How so?" Her tone betrayed the small spike of irritation igniting in her stomach. It had been years since someone had commented on the way she lived her life. She didn't think he knew her well enough to be making such a statement.

"Early to the clinic, staying late, no time off, no longer doing your photography. Do I need to go on?"

Who did he think he was to be saying something like that to her? "I don't need you telling me how I should live."

"I'm just making an observation." He bit into a cool chip, making a loud crunching sound. "I don't think anyone could make you do anything you don't want to."

"It sounded like an accusation to me."

"I didn't mean for it to. I just think you need to take better care of yourself."

"Do you make it a habit of cooking for people and then telling them how they need to live their lives?"

He cocked his head, saying nothing for a moment as if in deep thought. "No-o-o." He drew the word out. "I don't think I've ever done it before." He sounded astounded that he had this time. "I guess you're just special that way."

The puppy chose that moment to nose around their feet. Taylor scooped up the small ball of fur in his large hand. With a long index finger he stroked the small head between the ears. The puppy snuggled into his lap. The contrast between the broad-shouldered man and tiny trusting animal captured her whole attention.

What would it be like to be on the receiving end of a tender touch from this man?

Taylor was running late the next morning. He hurried to the car. He stopped short in the humid air when he saw that Shelby's truck was still parked behind his car.

Something must be wrong. He'd been there a little over a week and Shelby had always been gone by the time he'd left for the clinic. He loped to the back door and up the outside steps. Shaking his head to think she didn't lock her doors, he pulled the screen door open and called, "Shelby?"

Listening, he heard a movement from the direction she'd gone the night before to change her shirt. He'd almost lost control when she'd returned from bathing the dog all wet and flushed, an enormous smile of pleasure on her face. He'd felt like he'd been sucker-punched, she'd been so beautiful.

Only by sheer willpower had he managed to make light of the situation. As soon as their meal had ended, he'd left before he did something he'd regret.

Now he headed to the bedroom that he'd been so tempted to find last night.

"Shelby, where are you?" His heart picked up speed as his concern increased. Why wasn't she answering?

A low whimper came from the room at the end of the hall and he went in that direction. If the puppy was here, Shelby would be nearby. Slowly pushing the bedroom door open, he called, "Shelby, are you okay? Can I come in?"

Receiving no response, he stepped farther into the room. The dog tried to climb out of the box next to the bed. Taylor lifted him into his arms. "So what have you done with Shelby, boy?" He rubbed the dog behind his ears. The puppy licked at Taylor's fingers as he looked at the bed. The only thing that might be Shelby was a large lump under the light blanket.

"Shelby, are you under there?"

Slowly the ball in the center of the bed began to move.

Relief filled him. At least she was alive. "What's wrong? It's past time to be at the clinic."

A groan and then "Oh, no" came from beneath the covers. Shelby pushed the pastel pink blanket back enough so that he could see her face.

Her hair went every direction as if she had been tossing and turning most of the night. A pale face and bloodshot eyes told him she was sick.

Taylor sat on the edge of the bed, the dog in the crook of one arm. "Shelby, you look awful." Maybe that wasn't the best example of his bedside manner but her misery took him by surprise.

"Get out. I'll get dressed and see you at the clinic," she said in a weak voice.

"How long have you been ill?"

"Since around midnight."

Her glassy-eyed look tore at his heart. "Ah, honey, you should've called me."

If she hadn't looked so pitiful, he would've laughed at her expression of disbelief. It had never occurred to her to call him for help. That hurt. He wouldn't let himself examine why it was significant.

"It's just a stomach virus. All I need is a shower and I'll feel better."

Taylor didn't move from the bed.

"Please leave."

"Are you sure you can make it to the shower without help?"

"I can take care of myself."

"Okay. I'll take Buster to the kitchen and feed him."

"Buster?" She looked at him in question.

"Yeah. I can't keep calling him 'Dog.' You yell if you need help."

He was confident she wouldn't be doing that no matter how terrible she felt. Shelby wouldn't admit any feebleness, to him or anyone else.

Taylor pulled the door shut but remained in the hall until he heard the shower running. He'd see that Buster got his breakfast then come back to check on Shelby.

By the time he returned, the water was no longer running. He knocked on the bedroom door but received no reply. Pushing it open, he didn't see Shelby. "You okay?" Still nothing. Going to the door of the bath, he knocked lightly. He couldn't take a chance that in her weakened state she'd fallen.

An unintelligible murmur came from the other side of the door. Concern overriding any other thought, Taylor didn't wait for an answer before going in.

Shelby sat on the edge of the tub wrapped in a towel, with her wet head against the aqua tile wall. She had taken a hot shower by all the steam floating near the ceiling. Her illness and shower combination had zapped what little energy she'd had left.

"Let me dry your hair and then I'll get you back into bed." Under any other circumstances that would have been a suggestive statement.

"I can do it. Just leave me alone."

"For crying out loud, Shelby, just this once accept some help. Now, you sit right there while I see about your hair." He pulled a towel off the holder.

"Give it to me. I'll do it."

Taylor looked at her meaningfully and briskly rubbed her hair with the towel. "Where's your hairdryer?"

After a long moment she pointed to the cabinet under the sink. *Stubborn woman.* Taylor quickly retrieved the appliance, plugged it in and sat down beside her. Being a novice hairdresser, this job was way outside his comfort zone but he'd do his best. He turned on the dryer and directed the air flow towards her head. His fingers gently ran though the wet strands, separating her hair into sections.

"Lean against me so I can get underneath." Giving her no opportunity to argue, he guided her head to his chest.

She rested against him but never completely relaxed. Didn't the woman ever think she could use someone's help? As her hair dried it became warm silk flowing through his hand. Could anything be sexier? He rubbed his cheek against the glossy cloud.

He turned off the dryer. She slowly sat up. Did she ever let go? Stop being obstinate? "Shelby, honey, you need to get dressed."

She looked at him weakly. He stood and put the hairdryer away. On the corner of the vanity he found a lacy gown that would have made his blood sizzle had circumstances been different. With it suspended on his index fingers by the tiny straps he asked, "You need help with this?"

"I can do it," she said, sounding stronger than she looked.

Relief filled him. And disappointment. It

would've been difficult to treat her as a patient if her luscious body had been on display. Still, it would've been his chance to see what he'd been daydreaming about for days.

He stepped into the bedroom but didn't completely close the door between them. Fear that she might fall kept him close. When she opened the door he scooped her into his arms, cradling her close.

She made a weak movement of protest. "Put me down."

He tightened his arms. As if she had no more energy to fight, she accepted his care and settled against him. "I assure you I have no intention of taking advantage of a woman when she's sick. I like my women willing and able, and obviously you're neither. So quit being so uncooperative. The sooner I have you tucked into bed the sooner I can get to the clinic."

"I need to go to work." She resisted his hold again.

"Not today you don't."

"But—"

"There's no but. I'll take care of the clinic. You need to rest."

"You can't tell me what to do."

"I can and I am. Doctor's orders."

"I have patients to see."

"Really, Shelby. Be reasonable. You don't want to give your patients whatever you have."

The fight left her. No matter what, she thought of her patients first, even before herself.

Taylor placed her on the sheets. Her short gown left an enticing amount of leg showing, forcing him to suppress a groan. He'd always remained a professional when taking care of a patient but seeing to Shelby was testing his restraint. For the first time he was having a difficult time keeping his actions and reactions strictly professional.

He pulled the floral sheet up, concealing the silken skin that his fingers itched to touch. He needed to leave before he did something she wouldn't appreciate and he'd regret.

Brushing her hair away from her face, he said, "I'll take Buster with me to the clinic. We'll be back to check on you at lunchtime."

Shelby feeling miserable made him feel the same. Taylor stopped at the door to the hall and looked back at her. Her breathing had already become steady and deepened.

Never before had Taylor resented his work but this time he wished he could spend the entire day sitting beside Shelby, nursing her back to health. The tiny dynamo had slipped into a corner of his life where he had never let another person go.

Shelby rolled over and looked at the clock on her bedside table. Eleven. She couldn't believe she'd slept the morning away, even though she'd been up most of the night. It had been a long time since she'd felt so wretched.

The clinic!

She flipped the covers back and sat up. Her head spun. Lying back, she flung an arm over her eyes. In the four years the clinic had been open, she'd not missed a day of work. As horrible as she felt physically, it killed her to know that she had patients needing to be seen.

No, Taylor was there. He was taking care of her patients.

Doing her work. Seeing that the community had medical care. She'd not relied on anyone in years, and she had to depend on him, of all people. She fought the rising panic the thought brought to her. The person who swore he was leaving as soon as he could, and she had to trust him.

Removing her arm from her eyes, she slowly sat

up. Her stomach rose and fell in protest. Maybe if she ate something she'd feel better. Placing a hand over her stomach, she made her way to the kitchen. She was standing on her toes taking the soda cracker box off the top cabinet shelf when the door opened. With a squeak she dropped the box. "Don't you know to knock?"

Taylor entered, carrying the dog. "I thought you'd still be in bed. From the look of things you should be."

"Thanks for making me feel better." She retrieved the box and placed it on the counter.

"I'll say I'm sorry if you'll promise to dress like that for me when you feel good."

Trying to overlook his statement, she said, "Hey, shouldn't you be at the clinic instead of here? What if someone comes? I'll get dressed."

"Relax, I left a note that I'd be back at one. You know you can train people to come to the clinic during the hours you set, don't you? You need a lunch hour. Your number is on the door if there's an emergency. Otherwise they can wait."

She couldn't ignore the heat of desire that became evident in Taylor eyes, which stopped further argument from her. His eyes had turned dark and daring. He put Buster down and stepped toward her. The dog's tail wagged as he found his food bowl.

Not expecting anyone to come into her house unannounced, she'd not put on a robe. Now she stood in front of Taylor in her thinnest, shortest gown. She was just short of naked. By the way he was looking at her she might as well have been. "A gentleman would turn his back and let me get something to cover up with," she said with as much authority as a queen as she headed toward her bedroom.

"A gentleman would but I've never been accused of being one," he called.

Shelby returned to the kitchen to find Taylor pouring something into a small boiler. Surprisingly, sparring with Taylor had made her forget about her stomach troubles. Now it complained more from hunger than a sour feeling. "What're you doing now?"

"I brought you lunch. Home-made chicken soup," he said as he stirred the soup.

"Home-made? When've you had time to make chicken soup? You did open the clinic, didn't you?" Her voice held a note of alarm.

"Yes, I've seen patients this morning. Mrs. Stewart came in to have her sciatica checked and asked where you were. To make a long story short, she said she'd make some chicken-noodle soup."

"With her leg problem, you asked her to make soup for me?"

He did have the decency to look contrite. "I didn't ask. She volunteered. I thought her soup would be better than something out of a can."

"That's sweet of her."

"Now sit down before you fall down while I get this heated."

Once again Taylor was busy preparing a meal for her. Jim had done little if any domestic work during their marriage. His total focus had been the clinic. Much like how it had now become her sole interest.

It hadn't taken Taylor the "I'm leaving town as soon as I can" man long to feel comfortable in her kitchen. He moved around the room with easy grace, finding the utensils and bowls with ease. Somehow it seemed natural, even reassuring to have him there. It was nice to have someone taking care of her. She'd almost forgotten how it felt.

Sitting in a chair, she picked up Buster and brought his face up to hers. "So what've you been doing all morning, little guy?"

"He spent most of the time in a box in your office. The rest of the time he spent eating. He can really put it away."

She settled Buster in her lap and he fell asleep. "That's what happens when you've been starving. You never seem to get enough." Kind of like she couldn't seem to get enough of Taylor's attention. Oh, that was heartbreak waiting to happen.

Taylor's gaze met hers. Did he think she was talking about something else?

When had she become so self-sufficient that she no longer needed a man in her life? She hadn't realized until recently that she'd been starving for a man's notice. Her days were spent giving others care but no one had taken the time to be concerned about her. Until today. Until Taylor. It was a heady feeling she'd miss when he left. The man was slipping in under her defenses.

Taylor placed two filled bowls on the table, and pulled the box of crackers out from under his arm. He went back and returned with two large glasses of iced tea.

"I don't know if my stomach can handle all this," she said, looking at the full bowl of soup.

"You need to eat something or you'll get dehydrated."

Dipping her spoon into the liquid, she put it in her mouth. "Mmm. It tastes wonderful."

"Kind of a hot meal for the middle of the summer but I thought it might make you feel better."

"Thanks for doing this. It's really nice of you."

He shrugged. "Not a problem. Least I can do for my landlord."

A prick of disappointment touched her. So he was just being nice because she'd given him a place to stay for a couple of weeks. Had she been hoping for more? Pushing that disconcerting thought away, she asked, "Who did you see this morning?"

"Mr. Rogers came in with a cough. Mrs. Smith had plantar fasciitis. Mark Myers has a bad cold. The usual stuff."

"Did you do an X-ray of Mr. Rogers's lungs? Rule out pneumonia. He's eighty-five."

"I took good care of him." Taylor put down his spoon, sat back in his chair and looked straight at her. "I thought by now you'd quit questioning my abilities. Have I given you any reason to doubt me?"

She reached over and placed her hand on his forearm. The heat of him seeped into her. "I'm sorry. You didn't deserve that. You've done excellent work while you've been here. And I don't know what I would have done without you today."

Taylor rubbed the pad of his index finger across her cheek. "I bet that was hard for you to admit. I'm glad I was here to help." An emotion similar to shock crossed his face, as if he was surprised to hear himself utter those words. She was certainly surprised by them. It was the first time he hadn't acted like he had his car headed out of town.

His attention centered on her fingers as they trailed off his arm. Suddenly the large kitchen had turned small and intimate. The air between them vibrated with awareness. She returned to eating with a great deal of effort and concentration. Taylor stood and went back to the stove to refill his bowl.

"I'm feeling better. I should get dressed and go back with you."

Taylor wheeled around from the stove. "For someone so intelligent, you have some of the most bizarre ideas."

"I don't have bizarre ideas!"

"Do you honestly believe that you have any business at the clinic this afternoon?"

"Yes, I do. It my clinic. My responsibility."

"You're human. You got sick. Maybe even, despite how horrible the thought, you might one day like to take a day off."

"What I'm I suppose to do here? I'm feeling much better."

"How about something you enjoy? While I'm here, take advantage of me. After I'm gone it may be a while before you get more help." He returned to the table with his bowl in hand.

Shelby hated to admit it but he was right. She loved her work at the clinic but it had consumed her life. It had been wonderful to spend yesterday outside, taking pictures, she'd even liked Taylor's company. It had been the first real leisure day she'd taken since Jim had died. One that wouldn't have happened if it hadn't been for Taylor's insistence.

"I'd better get back," Taylor said, scooting his chair back having finished his meal. "Mrs. Ferguson is on the schedule for a blood-pressure check so I'd better be there to help her in."

Shelby smiled. The old woman wouldn't be happy to learn that Taylor would be caring for her again.

"What?" He stood and started stacking the used bowls.

"Just thinking you might be taking a liking to us."

"I just might be," he said, soft enough that she looked at him. "Some more than others."

His intense stare made her wonder if she was starting to run a fever.

"You're kind of growing on us too," she murmured.

He leaned toward her.

"Don't get too close. You might catch what I've got."

His mouth moved closer. "I'll take my chances."

She placed a hand on his chest, stopping him. "I don't think this is a good idea."

"You're probably right," he murmured as his arm came around her. His hand settled low on her back and he pulled her against him. "But I've wanted to do it for too long to stop now."

His lips were dry and firm as they met hers. At first he tested and teased. This kiss was nothing like the first one. It was different than any she'd ever experienced. So tender it could've been her very first kiss. She moved forward, resting against him, soaking up the heaven that was being in his arms.

The squeal of an animal in pain pierced the air.

She jerked back. She'd stepped on Buster's foot. Taylor's hands dropped away. The warmth and security of being next to him disappeared.

Taylor picked up the dog. "I get a chance to kiss a beautiful girl and you get in my way."

Beautiful girl. Taylor thought she was beautiful.

"Are you feeling well enough to have Buster for company this afternoon?" he asked, placing the dog on the floor again. "He wasn't as well behaved this morning as I had hoped."

"I think so." She forced herself to sound normal after that earthquake of a kiss. "We could both use a nap, I'm sure."

"Wish I could stay and join you," he said in a suggestive voice, along with a long passionate look, before abruptly turning and stepping through the screen door and letting it slam behind him.

How had he managed to reduce her to having a schoolgirl crush in only seven short days?

CHAPTER SIX

SHELBY woke from her nap feeling much improved. Bathing again, she dressed and styled her hair. With a surprise she realized that it had been nice to get some rest without worrying about the clinic. For at least today the concerns of the clinic had been Taylor's and that was a freeing feeling. She could too easily get used to not carrying all the burdens in her life.

Now she sat at her desk, with Buster asleep on a towel beside her. She'd love to spend more afternoons this way. Pushing a button on her computer, she brought up the pictures she'd taken the day before. She clicked on each individual photo in the rows of small squares. With one tap a photograph of Taylor standing causally in front of the shack filled the screen.

Even his picture made her blood hum. He was a handsome man with high cheekbones and a strong jaw. That she was well aware of already. His well cared-for appearance contrasting against the dilapidated building made him the focal point of the photo. He captivated her by simply looking into the camera.

Thoughts of his kisses made her heart break the speed limit. She shouldn't let that happen again. It would be too easy to let him into her heart. But what then?

She clicked through each picture. It wasn't until the picture where he'd looked directly at her that the veneer slipped. There his vulnerability became visible. No doubt he'd not meant for that particular part of his personality to show. Aware of his need, she longed to soothe him.

"Hey, what're you doing?" Taylor interrupted her thoughts.

Shelby squealed, her hand going to her chest. "For heaven's sake, Taylor, are you trying to scare me to death?"

"I thought for sure you would've heard the door slam."

Buster made a whimpering sound and Taylor picked him up.

"So, I see you're feeling better. What are you up to?"

"Just looking over the pictures I took yesterday."

"Mind if I see?"

He pulled a chair up before she could respond. "Scoot over."

Now he was entirely too close for her comfort. She went back and began clicking through the photos. The house and surrounding landscape had turned out perfectly. Taylor made noises of appreciation and interest in his throat. A soft, warm feeling washed over her at each of his responses.

She leaned back in the chair and put her hands in her lap.

"What about those?" he pointed to the last row of pictures.

"They're just more of the house."

"I'd like to see them also."

With a resigned sigh she put the cursor over the first picture. His face popped into focus.

He moved nearer and gently pushed her hand off the mouse and continued clicking. "Why didn't you want me to see these?"

"I don't know. I thought they might make you feel uncomfortable."

"Why? You're an excellent photographer. Didn't you think I would like them?"

She shifted in the chair because of both his earnest question and him being so near. "I wasn't sure." Did he not see what she did?

Taylor stopped on the one where he'd been watching her, really watching. He studied it for a long moment before he sat back and said, "You have a real talent. One you should be sharing with the world."

She huffed.

He smiled. "Okay, at least this part of the country. You should see about setting up a show." His eyes widened and he lightly slapped his leg. "You know, it would be a great way to raise awareness and money for the clinic. Bring reality to the need for clinics like Benton's."

"I don't think so. I'm not that good and I certainly don't have time to prepare for something like that. The clinic has to come first." She leaned back.

"That's the point." He leaned toward her, his eyes earnest. "You could help the clinic while you're also taking care of yourself. You need to get away from work some."

Rolling her chair away from the computer and Taylor, she stood and faced him. The stab of anger and something else she wouldn't name rose again in her stomach. "I don't need you telling me what to do. If you're so interested in helping, maybe you should commit to staying here and working at the clinic indefinitely, or at least until I find someone to replace you."

Taylor stood, looked at her from across the room. "I've made it clear that I can't do that. I'm only here because your uncle gave me no real choice. Stop trying to drag me into something I want no part of!"

"Is it can't or won't? What would be so awful about having to live here for a little while longer? You seem to be doing fine. And people are starting to like you."

"Enough pushing!" he snapped, and headed out the door.

Taylor normally didn't care when someone was aggravated with him. After years of living with his father's drunken tirades, he'd learned to tune out people's negative emotions. Regardless of that discipline, the tension between Shelby and himself was starting to get to him. For some reason, her happiness mattered.

Why it was important he couldn't comprehend. He never let anyone get close enough for their feelings to affect him one way or another. He wished he could give her what she wanted but he couldn't. Making his life in Benton wasn't possible. Was he even capable of having a positive relationship with someone?

He'd worked too hard to gain his self-respect, and the respect of others. Now if people were talking about him, it was because of his skill as a doctor, not because he was the brainy son of the town drunk. This tiny town brought back bad memories and he refused to live with them even for Shelby's sake. Still she pushed against that well-established barrier he'd built to protect his emotions. That wall was swaying. He was afraid that if she continued to shove, the partition would fall. Then he'd be vulnerable to a pain greater than any he'd ever known.

Carly knocked on the office door, drawing his attention away from his turmoil. The paperwork he'd been trying to catch up on during a lag in patients that afternoon might have to wait.

"Yes?"

"You have a patient. I put him in exam one," she said.

"Thanks. I'll be right there."

As he opened the door of the exam room, he

glanced at the chart for a name. "So, uh, Bill, what seems to be wrong?"

He looked up to find a boy of around ten sitting on the exam table. He was battered and bruised about the face and one sleeve of his shirt had been torn. One knee was badly skinned and the other was openly bleeding. A small trail of blood went down his shinbone.

The boy had been in a fight. He'd not been the winner. Taylor knew the blank look in the boy's eyes. Had seen it in the mirror countless times. Torment gripped Taylor like a strap squeezing his chest.

"What happened?" Taylor had to work to keep his voice steady.

"Some boys at school beat him up," said the haggard-looking mother standing beside the exam table.

"Tell me what happened," Taylor said as he gathered supplies. He would do what his training had taught him to do for now. Later, he'd try to forget.

"It has been an ongoing problem. Some of the boys won't leave him alone. They tease him. He won't let me talk to the kids' parents. Doesn't want me to talk to the teachers. Then this happened." The woman looked at Taylor with tearful eyes.

Taylor knew the feeling well. He'd been hit a number of times before his mother had found out. He wasn't sure his dad ever had. "The school authorities know?"

"Yes, they sent us here." She thrust a paper at him. Taylor glanced at it and set it aside.

"If this continues I'll have no choice but to contact the police."

The boy's eyes widened. Fear filled the blank look that had been in his eyes. Taylor wouldn't be the one giving the report. He was only going to be there a few more days.

Taylor finished examining the boy, relieved there were no broken bones or internal bleeding, then applied bandages to his knee. "You'll need to keep ice on that eye. Twenty minutes on and twenty minutes off."

The mother nodded.

"Now I'd like to speak to Bill for a minute, if you don't mind?" he addressed the mother, while forcing a smile to reassure the boy. Smiling was the last thing Taylor felt like doing. One little boy's troubles had transported him back to days in his life he'd like to forget.

The mother stepped outside the door and Taylor pulled the chair up in front of the boy. "Bill, I know how hard this is for you because I was once you. I fought at school too. But a man told me that if I did my best in school I could one day be better than all the boys who gave me a hard time. I did work hard in school and it gave me a chance to go to college. There I slowly became proud of myself, liked myself, and that made me stronger than those boys who had always been mean to me.

"So stay in school and make the best grades you can. One day you'll be stronger than those boys picking on you too. Knowledge is power. You never know, one day you might even be their boss and tell them what to do." Taylor pulled one of the leftover coupons out of his pocket. "Now, go get yourself an ice cream."

The slightest smile came to Bill's lips and the sadness disappeared briefly from his eyes.

Minutes after the boy and his mother left the clinic, Taylor stalked out to his car, climbed in, put the top down and headed out to nowhere in particular. He just had to get away. Find some way to ease that band of pain.

That kid's fearful, beaten and disillusioned look

tore at his gut. Taylor had worked hard to put those same horrific emotions behind him. That was a sham. All it took was one boy in one small town to make them return with a vengeance. He was still an inmate in the prison of his past. A childhood wasn't something he could make vanish. Somehow he had to learn to live with it or he would never be free of it.

Shelby searched the driveway from the kitchen window to see if Taylor had come home. Where was he? Surely he wouldn't have left town without saying goodbye, even if they'd had a disagreement.

She hadn't seen him all afternoon and the clinic was slow but even then they should've crossed paths. Finally she asked Carly if she'd seen him.

"He walked out with the little boy who'd been beaten up and his mother. I saw him get in his car and leave."

Taylor hadn't returned to the clinic by the time she'd locked up and his car hadn't been in the drive when she'd arrived home. He'd made it clear he wasn't interested in socializing with people who lived around here, so she couldn't imagine that he'd stopped at the local bar or was at a church event. Those were the only two places open in town that evening.

Now it was going on midnight and he'd still not shown up. Worry made her stomach tense. What had happened to make him leave so abruptly? To stay away?

She turned the light off over the kitchen sink to see more clearly. A misty rain fell and the red car hadn't returned to the drive. Had Taylor been in an accident? Was he in a ditch somewhere? He had a track record of driving too fast. What if he had skidded off the road and no one had seen him do it? A flash of Jim's car wrapped around the tree burst into her mind, but she shook off the image. As perturbed as she'd been with him for leaving without telling anyone, she still wouldn't want anything bad to happen to him.

A double beam of light skimmed across the glass. Shelby's heart rose and fell. The light straightened and then was extinguished. Taylor was home. Relief flooded through her and she was left with a nervousness that could only be the aftermath of fear.

Now she could go to bed.

Picking up the bed she'd bought for Buster, she walked through the dark house to her bedroom.

Placing the sleeping dog on the floor beside her nightstand, she took one last look out her back window at the garage.

Taylor stood at the window with the dim glow of a light behind him. His normally strong shoulders were hunched, his head down and hands shoved into his pockets. His body language was in complete contrast to the one she'd seen the last time he'd stood there. He looked like a man totally isolated from the world. Taylor was in pain. Everything about him screamed it.

His head rose and he looked in her direction. She held her breath. Did he know that she was watching him? He ran a hand through his hair and turned away.

Shelby slipped under the bed covers. She should be exhausted but sleep eluded her. What was going on with Taylor? She rolled over, hugging a pillow to her. Would he be there in the morning? She needed to know for the clinic's sake. If she was truthful, she needed to know for herself.

Unable to stand it any longer, she tossed the sheet off and stood. Pulling on shorts and a light sweatshirt over her shorty gown, she headed for the back door. When Buster whimpered, she scooped him up.

Light still burned in Taylor's window. The gentle rain turned heavier as she crossed the short distance to the steps. It began to pour as she climbed the stairs. She knocked on the door of the apartment, her head down against the deluge. She cradled Buster closer as her hand went up to knock again. Before knuckle met wood, the door swung open.

Taylor stood there in nothing but navy slacks. They hung on his hips and were zipped but not buttoned.

"Shelby, what are you doing here?"

Before she could respond, he took her by the upper arms and pulled her out of the rain. She stood inside the door while he stalked to the bathroom and returned with a towel. "Give him to me." He reached for Buster, swapping the towel for the dog. As she dried her head, Taylor placed the dog on another towel on the floor.

"I just wanted—" she started.

"This isn't a good time for a lecture about how I should be more considerate of the clinic," he snapped. His mouth drew into a tight line and he stood with his hands fisted at his side.

"I—"

"You need to leave, Shelby. Just leave me alone."

She couldn't. Shelby stepped toward him, her wet hair hanging in ropes about her head. The sweatshirt lay heavy with water across her shoulders.

"Let me tell you something, Taylor Stiles. My being here has nothing to do with the clinic." She stepped closer, poking her index finger into his chest. He remained immobile but his eyes narrowed. "I've been worried about you." Another poke. "Afraid you'd had an accident." Another poke. "I'm sorry I wasted my time."

At the next poke Taylor grabbed her hand and pulled her to him. She slammed against his chest. His mouth lowered, taking control of hers. Strong arms circled her waist, lifting her. His mouth eased, shifted and took possession more thoroughly. Heat flooded her, pooled low in her middle, making her tingle with longing.

Her hands skimmed across the warm skin of his chest over the strong column of his neck, before wrapping around it. Taylor felt strong, secure, steady. Something she'd missed for so long. She leaned into him.

His tongue teased the seam of her lips and she

opened for him, inviting him in. He swept her, teased her, and parried, asking her to play. Tentative at first, she joined him eagerly.

Taylor took the kiss deeper. One of his hands moved to cup her bottom, bringing her closer. Gradually he eased the kiss and his hands moved to grip her waist. He let her slowly slide down him. The evidence of his desire stood hard and prominent between them. When her feet touched his floor, he pushed her gently away.

"You should go."

This strong, intelligent man was a suffering soul and she had a soft spot for suffering souls. She couldn't leave him when he needed someone.

"No." She stood on trembling legs.

He moved to stand at the window, staring out into the night. She came up beside him, lifted a hand to touch his back.

"Don't," he growled.

She pulled her hand away. "Taylor, you need to talk."

"I want to do something more than talk with you." His voice carried a gritty sound of need.

"I know," she said softly. "I'm here. Please tell me what's wrong. You're scaring me."

Taylor hung his head. No one had worried

about him in so long. He'd never allowed him-self to dream that Shelby might. Could he explain his feelings to her? Would she understand? Dared he think she really cared?

Her fingertips were like points of fire on his skin when she touched his back. Gently the palm of her hand came to rest flat on him and moved in a soothing pattern.

"Tell me what's wrong. I want to help." Shelby continued her tender caress. "What happened today? Why did you leave?"

As her hand moved across his skin he felt his muscles relaxing, his breathing slowing.

"The kid that came in today had been bullied at school." *Just say it and get it over with then she'll leave.* "That was me. I was the kid of the town drunk. Which gave them a lot of material. As a little kid it was a daily occurrence until I started defending myself. That led into fights and esca-lated into rebelling against everything and every-one. It became a big ugly circle of pain. One that I don't want the kid I saw today to live through."

The movement of her hand faltered for a sec-ond. Her calming movement started again with more pressure from her fingertips. Her arms en-circled his waist, her face coming to rest against his back. Dampness touched his skin. Shelby was crying for him! When had anyone cried for him?

He turned and enveloped her in his arms. Her face rested against his chest. She snuggled into him as if she wanted to absorb his pain. "Sweetie, don't cry. That was a long time ago."

"I'm crying for that boy that had to live with so much heartache."

He pulled her more securely against him. Her arms around his waist squeezed him closer. He'd never felt more humbled. This woman who had experienced great loss and worked herself almost beyond what was humanly possible was crying for a little boy she hadn't even known. What had he done to deserve her concern? Some of the pain of being an outsider with no one who really cared about him slowly seeped from him.

"I've seen kids in the ER numerous times who'd been beaten but none got to me like this boy. I've kept my childhood issues closed off for years, pushed them away as I focused on first med school then my career. I didn't even bring them out to examine when I had no family at my graduations, or spent my holidays alone. It just was. I accepted that. Until today, when they just came boiling out. I had to leave, take some down time. I'm sorry if I left you in the lurch."

He sucked in a breath at the soft touch of her lips on his chest. Seconds later, the brush of her mouth against him made him forget the past and concentrate fully on the here and now. Shelby was in his arms.

Her hands began to travel over his back, stopping to knead before moving on to explore another spot.

"Shelby? Do you know what you're doing?" His breath spurted unevenly against her hair.

"Mmm… Comforting you?" She nipped at his skin and his manhood stiffened.

Hands on her shoulders, he pushed her far enough away to meet her gaze. "I'm not interested in your pity. Admit it, you want me."

His skin rippled across his back as she trailed her fingers down to his waist and up over his pecs to his neck.

Standing on tiptoe, she stretched upwards. "I thought I was making that clear."

"I want to hear you say it."

"I want you," she whispered over his lips before they met his.

Need, strong, bottomless and more frightening than he'd ever experienced, filled him.

What was she doing? Shelby had never been the aggressor in lovemaking. But Taylor needed her. That little boy in him who'd lived daily in misery and the grown man who'd overcome so much touched her heart. She grieved for the boy and hurt for the scarred man.

He met her tentative kiss with one of fire, consuming her. His tongue entered, demanded. She accepted and gave. Fanning her fingers though his hair, she pulled his head closer. Heavenly, hot, hungry moments later his lips left hers to skim along her cheek, leaving butterfly kisses behind. His mouth traveled down her neck. She shivered.

"We need to get this damp shirt off you," he murmured against her neck as his hands went to the hem of the garment.

She raised her hands above her head, allowing him to slip the shirt off. He dropped it to the floor and pushed her shorts over her hips and down, leaving her standing in her gown.

His index finger followed the line of lace that covered her right breast to where it ended at her cleavage. Her nipples puckered in response. His finger moved to tease the nipple of her left breast. A quake of delight ran through her.

"As much as I like this little slip of clothing, I know I'll like what's under it so much more," he said in a low gravelly voice that made her tremble.

Before she could respond, she stood naked before him.

"Mercy, you're beautiful." He bent his head and took her nipple into his mouth. His tongue teased and tugged just as he had done with his kisses. Her center melted, ready for him. There was an excitement to being in Taylor's arms that she'd never known existed between a man and a woman, despite her years of happy marriage. He moved to her other breast, giving it the same undivided attention. She shifted toward him, sliding her hands over his shoulders to prevent herself falling.

He chuckled lightly. "Like that, do you?"

Putting her hands on each side of his head, she encouraged him to meet her look. "I do, but I think before we go any further you should turn off the light. We've probably already given the neighbors the show of a lifetime."

He reached over and clicked off the floor lamp,

leaving only the light from the bathroom, which prevented them from being in total darkness. Taking her hand, he led her towards the bed.

"What about the bathroom light?"

"No, I want to see you. I don't care what the neighbors know."

She didn't either. What she cared about was him.

He pulled the bedcovers away and she sat on the bed, tugging his hand to encourage him to join her. Instead of coming with her, he resisted, letting go of her hand. She scooted back, watching in fascination and anticipation as he unzipped his slacks and let them drop to the floor.

Taylor was all proud male, his desire evident. For her. There was a potent power in knowing she had such an effect on him.

Placing a knee on the edge of the bed, he leaned over and kissed her. She reached for him. He came down but instead of covering her, as she wanted, he lay on his side, his head supported by a hand. What began as a protest turned to a sharp intake of breath when he trailed his free hand over her hip bone and followed the curvature of her waist upwards.

She quivered as he continued his exploration

by tracing the arc of one breast before tugging gently at a straining nipple. He then focused his attention on her other breast that ached for his devotion. Her breath came roughly and raggedly. Heat filled her, making her squirm.

"I love the way you respond to me," he said with a voice full of wonder. He lifted and tested the weight of her breast before his hand moved lower across her stomach.

"Taylor, please," she said, rolling her hips towards him.

"Please. I like the sound of that word coming from you."

"Don't tease." She pushed his shoulders to the bed and straddled him.

"Imagine you wanting to be in charge." His chuckle rumbled low in his chest but held a note of excitement. "This time I think I'll enjoy it."

She came up on her knees then bent to give him a wet, hot kiss, letting her breasts graze his chest. The moan of a man teetering at the edge of his limit filled the air. She smiled against his lips and he took control of the kiss.

His tongue circled her mouth, asking and demanding and tempting. One of his hands fondled a breast while the index finger of the other hand found her center. His finger slowly entered her, retreated and went deeper the next time. She gasped, absorbed the pleasure and begged for more.

Shifting, Taylor rolled Shelby over onto her back and followed her. She boldly met his gaze and offered herself.

The woman in his arms was killing him. She kept such a tight rein on her world yet she was so sweetly, and without reservations, offering her beautiful body to him. What had he done to deserve his dreams coming true? He reached for his wallet on the bedside table, found the small packet and covered himself.

Returning his focus to Shelby, he watched her expressive dove-gray eyes go from yearning anticipation to contemplation to exhilaration as he sheathed himself within her heat. Her eyes slowly closed. She whispered his name and he smiled. He thrust deeper and she met him with a lift of her hips in acceptance. His world rocked, never to be the same again.

Kissing her tenderly while giving her the pleasure she craved, he found his own but at the same time lost his heart.

Later Taylor lay back, pulling the warm sleeping Shelby more snugly against him. He didn't regret making love with Shelby. How could he? It was the closest to heaven he'd ever been.

Yet what had he done? This wasn't a quick fling. This was the real thing. The thing he'd thought he'd never have, could never have. He still couldn't.

Shelby had said she and her husband had moved to Benton with the idea of having a family. Could he offer her the same? What kind of father would he be? He had no experience in that area. Worse, he'd had no example to follow. Was it possible for him to move beyond how he'd been raised? Surely he could do a better job of parenting than his father? Anyone could.

But what he was confident of was that Shelby would accept no half-measures. She desired a family—had told him that was her dream—and would settle for nothing less than a lifetime.

It wasn't yet light outside when Shelby woke to an arm heavy across her waist and a hand cupping a breast. A shockwave of contentment ran through her. Taylor didn't even have to be awake for her body to react to him being near. It had been a long time for her, and Jim had been her only one, but Taylor had loved her with such tenderness and so thoroughly she'd never felt a moment of apprehension. Her pleasure had seemed to be his only concern. She shifted slightly and the hand pulled her tighter against the solid wall of maleness behind her.

"Don't," his husky voice whispered against her ear, before his mouth lightly tugged at her earlobe. "Too nice here."

She rolled over and kissed him. "I'm not going anywhere. Just getting more comfortable."

The reality of the hurt she'd opened herself up to washed over her. She may not be going anywhere, but he'd be leaving soon. And it might kill her when he did. He'd only been there a short while but he'd managed to ingratiate himself so undeniably into her life, her heart that she might not recover from the loss.

"What's wrong?" Taylor asked, propping his head on a hand and looking down at her.

Had she made a movement or sound betraying her distress or was he so cognizant of her emotions that he sensed what she was feeling? If the latter was the case, she'd have to work hard to keep her thoughts from being transparent. She had to distract him. Was there more to his story than he'd told her?

"I was just wondering…" she trailed her hand across his chest and kissed a spot over his heart "…if you'd tell me about yesterday. What happened?"

Taylor flopped backwards on the bed and looked up at the ceiling. When she moved closer, he put an arm loosely around her. She sighed. He wasn't pushing her away.

"Do you really want to hear all the ugly details?"

She pulled the sheet up over them and then placed her head on his chest. His heartbeat was steady beneath her ear but the tension in his body said there was nothing calm about him.

"Where did you go?" she whispered.

"Just around."

"You drove around for eight hours."

"Yeah."

Shelby barely heard the word it was said so softly. She sat up, bringing a corner of the sheet up with her, covering herself. Her movement left much of Taylor exposed to her view. Heaven help her, he was gorgeous. As much as she enjoyed his body, she still needed to understand him. She wanted to help him through whatever was hurting him. At least she could give him that before he left.

"Please tell me why."

He took a deep breath. His body shuddered as he released it. "I've already told you more than I've ever told anyone else."

"We all have something negative in our past. Why is it a secret?"

"Not a secret, just not something I enjoy talking about."

"I would like to understand."

"It wasn't the best time in my life."

She placed a hand on his forearm in encouragement. The muscles under her hand jumped.

"I was the youngest of the town drunk's three sons. My mother worked herself into an early grave cleaning houses and whatever else she could find to do to keep clothes on our backs and food on the table. She died when I was sixteen."

"I'm so sorry, Taylor." As if he hadn't heard her, he continued. His eyes seemed to focus on the gloomy night outside.

As if lost in his memories, his voice became a monotone. "The kids at school were particularly cruel. The teachers tried to help. But there was nothing they could really do. I was too angry.

If I'd been a jock it might have been better but I stayed in so much trouble I never qualified for any school team. The only thing I had going for me was that school was easy for me."

She reached out to him, began to say something.

He pushed her hand away. "No. I don't need your sympathy. I've moved on. I have a completely different life now."

It stung that he didn't want her comfort. What he didn't see was that he hadn't really moved on. His past still controlled him. He still saw himself as that ne'er-do-well child he'd been told he would be.

"Are your father and brothers still living?"

"I heard that my father died while I was in college. I've not talked to my brothers in years. When I left for college they were on their way to becoming my father. I got my chance to get out of town and I've not been back." Bitterness surrounded each of his words.

"So what gave you your chance to leave?"

Couldn't he see that it was cathartic for him to be letting go after years of holding the disappointment and hurt inside? Glad she could be there for him, she waited.

"An old man telling me to use my brains instead of my fists made the difference. I did. My high-school counselor noticed me, knew my background, saw my grades and helped me with scholarships to college."

He said the last statement with a finality that said she shouldn't ask any additional questions. Instead, she wrapped her arms around his waist, settled her head on his chest and hugged him close. She wanted to absorb his painful memories, make them fade.

Long seconds ticked by before Taylor returned her embrace. Gently he rolled her over and brought his lips down to hers, letting her warmth push the coldness of the past away.

CHAPTER SEVEN

TAYLOR lightly rubbed his cheek against Shelby's soft hair as she lay nestled against his shoulder. He watched as the pink of the new morning edged the top of the large oak tree in her neighbor's yard. Having Shelby in his arms and a beautiful sunrise was the perfect way to start any day.

He'd learned early to accept what life dished out. This time he recognized that making love with Shelby had been a mistake. A wondrous, soul-touching mistake. He couldn't return to a town like the one he'd grown up in. He'd worked too hard to get out. No matter how much he cared for Shelby or how much he was needed here as a doctor, neither were strong enough to entice him to call this place home. He wouldn't break his promise to himself.

Shelby deserved better than what he could give her. She needed someone beside her who shared the same hopes and dreams. Who knew how to be a husband. A father. He wasn't that person.

In the long run he'd only make her unhappy. He didn't want to live his life always on guard. No, small-town life wasn't for him.

The woman of his dreams shifted against him and leaned her head back. His gaze met her misty gray one. She blinked twice.

"Hi," she whispered, with a sweet smile on her lips.

"Hey, there." Unable to resist those lips, he kissed her lightly. The knowledge that this sexy, exciting and generous woman had given herself so totally to him made his heart swell with pleasure yet at the same time caused it to ache. He couldn't keep her.

"Shelby, we need to talk."

She tensed in his arms then pulled away, rolling to the side of the bed. The sheet dropped away, leaving an enticing view of her back and the curve of her well-rounded behind. The desire to run his hand along those smooth curves made his fingers flex against the sheet.

"I'm not interested in an uncomfortable morning-after discussion."

He grabbed her wrist, stopping her from standing. She didn't turn to him. "Shelby, I wish you'd look at me."

She half turned but didn't meet his eyes.

"You know nothing can come of this. I can't stay in Benton," he said quietly. "Just as I know you can't leave."

"That's a cop-out but I'm a big girl. I understand. I need to get ready to go to the clinic now." She stood and started dressing.

The tempting view of her naked body made him want to pull her back against him and kiss her until she forgot about the last few minutes. But her jerky movements as she pulled on her sweatshirt said she wouldn't tolerate being touched.

He'd hurt her. She had a right to be hurt. And it had been the last thing in the world he'd wanted to do.

When he'd needed someone, she'd been there. She'd given herself. Even cried for him. What had he done? Used her.

Slipping out of bed, he started gathering his clothes. The silence in the room hung as heavy as humidity in the hot southern summer. He wanted to go to her, reassure her, tell her all she wanted to hear, but he couldn't lie.

Disgust brought a sour taste in his mouth. He'd fulfilled the prophecy of his youth. He'd amounted to nothing when it mattered to someone he cared about.

"I'll see you at the clinic," she said as she closed the door on her way out.

She sounded too calm. As if she'd already relegated him to something in the past with no intention of ever giving him another thought. The urge to punch something flared in him.

Buster whimpered at his feet. He picked the dog up and scratched his belly. He'd finish out his time at the clinic. That he had no choice about but he'd try to keep his relationship with Shelby strictly professional. For both their sakes.

The tricky part was he couldn't think of anything more difficult to accomplish.

Shelby had thought her days long and stressful without help at work but they'd been nothing compared to what this morning brought. The tension between her and Taylor made working together almost intolerable.

The situation must be bad if Carly, a teen totally focused on her own world, asked what was going on. Shelby shrugged. "Nothing." A totally ineffectual lie.

Carly's nose wrinkled in disbelief. "Right."

"We need to get back to work."

"It had started to be fun to work here. You

smiled and laughed," Carly mumbled as she logged into the computer. "Now even Dr. Stiles is all about work. You two need to try some of that adult advice you're always handing out."

The door opened with a jingle of a bell.

"That's enough, Carly," Shelby said repressively.

Mrs. Ferguson waddled towards them.

"Hello, what can we do for you today?" Shelby asked as she mustered a smile she'd didn't feel.

"I'm just stopping by to see that Dr. Stiles. He insisted I come by to have my blood pressure checked again."

"Do you want me to do it or would you rather see Dr. Stiles."

"I guess I might as well see him, since he's the one that told me to come in," Mrs. Ferguson said gruffly.

It seemed Shelby wasn't the only one who was starting to take a liking to Taylor.

"Carly, please let Dr. Stiles know that Mrs. Ferguson is here," Shelby said.

The girl didn't try to hide her surprise. Shelby had instructed her after the first day when she'd fallen all over herself to help Taylor that her job was to stay behind the deck.

The phone rang and Carly hesitated, looking at Shelby questioningly. "You get the phone. I'll find Dr. Stiles."

In reality, Shelby didn't have to hunt for Taylor. She knew where he was. She'd been aware of his movements all day. Her body hummed with the thought of him. She'd never given herself so totally to a man.

He'd taken what she'd offered but he'd freely given in return.

She wasn't angry with him, disappointed if anything but even that wasn't rational. He'd done nothing to deserve either of those responses. Did she really think that one night of passion would make him change his mind? She'd been the one who'd gone to his apartment. If she was angry with someone it should be herself. She'd created her own heartache.

The door to what was now their shared office stood open. Taylor had managed to carve out an area on the desk for his own pens and personal items. It amazed her that she'd so easily permitted him space. This room was her sanctuary, the door she closed on the world. Not even Carly came into this room freely. Stepping into the doorway, she found Taylor sitting behind the desk, staring off into space. Was he thinking about their discussion this morning or their lovemaking during the night?

"Taylor, Mrs. Ferguson is here." It didn't even bother her that the older woman was now more his patient than hers.

His gaze met hers. "Shelby—"

"Mrs. Ferguson is waiting." She didn't trust herself to say more when all she wanted to do was to walk into his arms and beg him to change his mind.

Shelby stepped into the lab. A minute later her body sent out a signal that Taylor stood nearby. Her hands shook as she placed the slide under the microscope.

"You can dodge me all you want," he said so softly he had to be standing right behind her, "but we will talk."

Twenty minutes after he left, she was preparing to call her next patient as Mrs. Ferguson came up the hall escorted by Taylor. The older woman stopped beside Shelby and placed a hand on her arm. "Honey, my kids have decided to give me a birthday tea this Saturday afternoon. I'd like you two to come." Mrs. Ferguson looked first at her and then at him.

Shelby glanced at Taylor. "I don't know if Dr. Stiles can make it. His work will be done here but I'll be there."

The words sounded catty even to her ears. She regretted them the second they were out.

Taylor's eyes narrowed, his brow wrinkled.

"Oh, are you leaving so soon?" Mrs. Ferguson's focus shifted to Taylor, oblivious to the stiffness between him and Shelby. "I had so hoped that you might decide to stay with us. I know Dr. Wayne has appreciated your help at the clinic. You'll be missed."

A flicker of shock entered his brown eyes and turned to a sparkle of pleasure. His face eased. He smiled at Shelby but spoke to Mrs. Ferguson, "I think I can hang around long enough to enjoy your birthday party."

"Good. It's being held in the church fellowship hall. Dr. Wayne can show you where to go. Now I must be going."

"I'll see you out." Taylor said, cupping the woman's elbow.

"I do love the personal touch I receive from my doctor," Mrs. Ferguson twittered.

Me, too.

* * *

Taylor finished his last charting chore and pushed the chair back from the desk. He and Shelby had swapped roles. Instead of her being the one to stay late, it was him.

As soon as it had been time to close the door for the day, she'd announced she was leaving. He was glad she was finely taking some time for herself, yet he knew it was also to put some space between them. He'd asked her to see to Buster. At least that had put a slight smile on her face. Taylor had gone home during lunch to check on the dog, but he needed to be let out to play that evening.

Refusing to spend another day like the one he had today, he had to clear the air between him and Shelby. He'd spent far too much time thinking about her and not enough focusing on his patients. He was grateful there hadn't been an emergency.

Even if he managed to get the stubborn, willful woman to listen to reason, could he keep his hands off her? Right now his body craved her touch, her warmth.

There were no lights on in or around her house when Taylor turned into the drive. Shelby's beat-up truck parked in the drive told him she was probably home. Maybe she'd gone to bed early? Was she out on a date? That latter question made his stomach clench. He didn't want Shelby seeing anyone, but he had no right to demand she didn't.

He walked toward his apartment and paused when he saw the dark form of Shelby sitting a couple of steps up on the stairs.

"Hi," she said so softly he almost missed hearing it above the noise from the night creatures talking to each other. "I've been waiting for you."

His heart fluttered. How he wanted her, wanted things to be right between them again.

"I need to apologize," she said in a steady, firm tone.

This wasn't what he'd been hoping for. By her tone of voice she wouldn't be sharing his bed tonight. How like her to meet the problem head on, though he didn't appreciate being considered an issue she had to solve. Being her knight in shining armor was more to his liking.

When he sat on the step below hers, she shifted her feet to one side to give him room. The riser was so short that one of her knees rested against his shoulder.

Having her touch, even in the slightest of ways,

gave him a feeling of belonging. Something he'd not realized he missed so profoundly until then. "You don't owe me an apology. We're two intelligent, consenting adults who spent the night together," he said. The untruth of the description screamed *You are so wrong* in his head seconds after he'd uttered it. It may have been the truth with other women in his life but not Shelby.

She wasn't just any woman. Shelby was *the* woman. The woman he could never make happy.

Her knee tensed against his shoulder. He'd hurt her—again.

"I understand. I'd just like to say I'm sorry for my very unprofessional remark in front of Mrs. Ferguson about you not staying for the party. It was uncalled for."

"Apology accepted."

She stood. "Well, I do appreciate all the help you've given me while you've been here."

"You're welcome." Their relationship had taken three giant steps backwards. Now they were talking to each other like they had when he'd first arrived. He didn't like this new stalemate. Could they ever recover the easiness they'd once known?

"Shelby—"

She walked down the stairs to the pavement, turned and looked back at him. "I'm tired and we both have a full day tomorrow. I've got Buster. Goodnight, Taylor."

He couldn't see her very well in the night shadows but the wistful tone in her voice came through loud and clear. A yearning to reach out and pull her back into his arms gnawed at him, but he couldn't let himself do it. He knew what hurt and rejection and wishing life to be different could do to a person. Adding to Shelby's pain wasn't something he was willing do.

Shelby made it just inside the kitchen door before tears slid down her cheeks. Until she'd said Taylor's name she'd believed she'd held herself together pretty well. The shake in the last syllable had given her away.

She'd tried to play the adult game of sex with no strings. She'd lost. She'd fallen and fallen hard for a man who refused to be a part of the town she'd made a pledge to. One she couldn't break. She and Jim had made a commitment to Benton to provide medical care. She'd promised Jim the night he'd died that she'd uphold their pledge, keep their dream alive. If she broke that vow,

she'd be dishonoring Jim's memory and everything she had spent the last few years working
towards. To have Taylor in her life, he had to embrace the town of Benton too, and all it meant
to her. In that tug of war, she wouldn't win. Taylor's childhood fears were stronger than his desire for her.

Heaving a sigh, she found her way to her bedroom and undressed without turning on the light.
The full moon that had risen over the trees shone
brightly enough that she didn't need to switch on
a lamp.

She couldn't resist the urge to look out the window at the apartment. There was no light on but
she knew with all her being that Taylor stood
there, looking down at her. A tingle ran though
her, leaving a path of longing deep and sharp. If
there was a silver lining in their whole mixed-up
relationship it was the knowledge that he seemed
as out of sorts as she.

With the faintest of movement the connection
was severed. Taylor was going to bed without her.

Some time later, a banging at her door brought
her out of her fitful sleep.

"Doc Wayne! Shelby!" a frantic voice yelled.

"I'm coming," she called.

Flipping on the lamp, she went to the closet and found her robe. Jerking it on and tying the belt, she made her way to the front door.

The beating and shouting continued. "I'm here. Hold on a minute," she called, turning on the porch light and opening the door.

"Sam, what's the problem? Why didn't you call me instead of waking the whole neighborhood?"

"The station tried but got no answer. They sent me."

She been so tied in knots after talking to Taylor that she'd left her phone on the kitchen table instead of taking it to the bedroom.

"What's going on here, Deputy?" Taylor asked from behind Shelby. She turned, her nose making contact with his bare chest. She glanced downwards to find him dressed in nothing but red plaid boxers. She groaned.

"We didn't mean to wake you. I can handle this," she hissed.

"I wasn't asleep." Taylor's deadpan tone said he was having as rough a night as she.

He must have seen the patrol car drive up, realized there was an emergency and come in through the back door. No matter why he was there, his appearance in her house to Sam and soon to the entire town it would look like they'd been sleeping together. She couldn't worry about that now.

Turning back to Sam, she saw the slight smirk on his face that confirmed her fears. "What's happened?" she asked the deputy in her most professional voice.

"There's been an accident on the Hartman farm. Something to do with a tractor. You're needed out there."

"I'll get dressed and get my bag. The ambulance service has been notified?"

"Yeah, but they're out on another run. They'll meet us there as soon as they can."

When she turned around Taylor was gone. She wasted no time wondering where he was off to. Instead she concentrated on the emergency ahead. She dressed in record speed in T-shirt, jeans, and tennis shoes, pulling a light jacket off a peg by the door. She also snatched up the emergency bag she kept stocked for these types of occasions. Reaching her truck, she found Taylor waiting with his own medical bag in hand. He took her larger bag and placed it in the back before then taking to the passenger seat.

As she climbed behind the wheel she said, "You don't have to come."

"Do you really think I'd let you go alone?" He sounded disappointed that she might think he would not do his duty. "We're a team," he said firmly.

What he'd left unsaid was "until the end of the week."

A little later Taylor stepped out of the truck onto the well-worn gravel of the drive circling in front of the farmhouse. The lights around the house blazed and a couple of large late-model trucks were parked off to the side. A police patrol car sat in front of the main door.

A middle-aged woman and a girl of about fourteen hurried down the steps trailed by a large dog. Sam, the deputy, followed them and came to stand beside Shelby.

"Dr. Wayne," the woman said, panic filling her voice, "I'm so glad to see you. Bob's leg is trapped."

"Trapped by what?" Taylor asked.

"Mrs. Hartman, this is Dr. Stiles. He's a trauma doctor from Nashville here helping me."

The woman nodded curtly and quickly turned her attention back to Shelby. "The tractor."

Shelby looked toward a large structure behind the house that had to be the barn. "Where is he?"

Mrs. Hartman pointed off into the distance. "Down in the bottoms near the river. He was trying to get in some last-minute bush hogging before the rain set in." Her words rushed together as she spoke. "He didn't come in at dark. I sent our son, John, to look for him. He found the tractor jackknifed. His dad is pinned in. John's down there with him right now. That private ambulance service is off on another run. It'll be awhile before they get here, and even then I'm not sure they can handle this. That's why I called you."

Sirens sounded in the distance. Shelby glanced at Sam. "Volunteer fire department," the deputy said. She dipped her chin in understanding.

"We need to prepare for shock, maybe puncture wounds, a break at the least," Taylor told her.

She nodded in agreement. "Mrs. Hartman, we're going to need blankets and towels. Is there someone who can show us where to go while you gather them?"

"My girl, Jenny, will take you."

"I'll wait for the fire department," Sam said.

The girl ran to a four-wheel flatbed vehicle with two seats. Taylor sprinted to the truck to retrieve the medical bags and met Shelby and the girl. "I'll sit on the back," he called. Shelby's look questioned his choice but for once she didn't argue. He climbed on and scooted on his bottom along the metal platform until his back was against the seats.

Jenny had the vehicle moving by the time he and Shelby were settled. They traveled through an open gate and into the darkness. As they left the yard behind the ride became bumpier. Due to the rough terrain, Taylor had a hard time telling where they were going or what the land looked like, with the beam of the headlights darting up and down. He had to hang onto the low metal bar to keep from sliding or falling off the flatbed.

"How far?" Shelby asked.

"Ten minutes," the girl said, before shifting into a higher gear and throwing them all sideways as one wheel hit a bump. Behind the two women, Taylor grabbed again for the metal bar. They traveled into the night as the all-terrain continued its slow, steady pace over the rough terrain.

With no real idea about what to expect, he could tell from Shelby's look earlier this wasn't going to be an easy case. The fact that they'd be working in the pitch dark wouldn't help.

Shelby glanced at him. Even in almost non-existent light, he could see her apprehension. He squeezed her shoulder gently. Was she worried she couldn't handle the situation? Or the blood?

Being a small-town kid, he had no experience with farms or farm equipment. His nerves were strained at the thought of what they might encounter.

They rode in silence for a while, following a track through the field and into a stand of trees. While fording a creek, they listed heavily to one side and then to the other as they rode over large rocks. He braced himself with both hands on either side of the vehicle to manage the sway. Using a leg, he was able to stop the med bags from sliding off.

"What kind of vehicle is this?" he asked the girl in a voice loud enough to be heard over the motor beneath him.

"An army mule."

"Mule?"

"It's some kind of World War Two thing."

Minutes later they came out of the woods and crossed a large field, approaching the scene of the accident. The only light present came from a four-wheeler's headlights pointed in the direction of the tractor.

From what he could tell, the tractor was an antique. It had a long body, with dual wheels close together in the front and large, head-high ones at the rear. Didn't these people own anything from the last decade?

One of the large wheels rested in a wide, three-foot ditch while the front wheels hung in the air. Behind it at a right angle was the bush hog pressed against the other back wheel. Sandwiched between the two pieces of dangerous equipment was Mr. Hartman.

"We're going to need to get more light down here," Taylor said.

"Neighbors are on their way with more four-wheelers." Even as Jenny said the words Taylor heard the whine of the vehicles. The girl pulled to a stop and he jumped off the mule, grabbing both bags. He paused long enough to see that Shelby had climbed down safely.

"Jenny, you go back and get those blankets and towels. Tell your mother to call the neighbors and to get a couple of tractors out here. Hurry back."

The girl hesitated.

"Your daddy's going to be fine," Shelby said,

standing on tiptoe to reach over and touch the girl's shoulder across the passenger seat. "You can help him best by helping us."

How like Shelby to not only take care of the patient but the family as well. In the big emergency room where he worked, he often never saw the family. The social worker did all the consoling.

"Shouldn't this be the EMTs' job?" Taylor asked as he and Shelby made their way over to the accident.

"Yeah, it would be if we had EMTs. We have a volunteer fire department and a private ambulance service. Nothing more. I'm the EMT on the rare cases like this."

A boy of about eighteen stood and came towards them from where he'd been sitting next to the injured man.

"John, I'm Dr. Wayne and this is Dr. Stiles. We're here to help your dad. We're going to get your father taken care of." At her reassuring words, the boy's shoulders relaxed.

He led them to where Taylor could see the man half lying, half sitting on the top of the bush hog, his body twisted in an unnatural position. Shelby fell to her knees beside the farmer. Taylor set the bags down and sat on one heel. Quickly, Shelby found a flashlight in the emergency bag.

"Mr. Hartman, you've managed to get yourself into quite a pickle this time." Shelby's bright tone played down the desperate situation. The man could lose his leg, possibly his life. "This is Dr. Stiles," she continued.

"Glad to see you, Doc," the man said weakly.

"Sorry it's under these circumstances." Taylor moved in close to Shelby as she shone the flashlight indirectly over Mr. Hartman's face. The man was already deathly pale. Pain lines circled his mouth.

"We're going to get you out of here as soon as we can. More help is on the way. While Dr. Stiles and I have a good look and listen to you, why don't you tell us what happened? Start with how long you've been here."

Taking the cue, Taylor reached for his own small bag, pulled out his stethoscope and began to listen to the farmer's heartbeat. It sounded thin but steady. His breathing sounds were what really concerned Taylor. They were rapid and shallow. Had he broken some ribs as he'd gone down? While Taylor worked, Shelby pulled out a small penlight to check the man's eyes. She then took his blood pressure.

"Been here since sunset." He paused, taking a breath. "Got too close to the ditch. Heard a noise. Sheer pin rattled loose. Tried to put spare in. Knew better. Stepped between the tractor and bush hog..." He paused, exhausted.

"Dad said that the ground below the right back tire gave away," John offered. "The tractor slid into the ditch, jackknifing the bushhog. He tried to jump backwards but didn't get his leg out in time."

"Well, that's quite a story, Mr. Hartman. You'll have something to tell your grandchildren one day," Taylor said, looping his stethoscope around his neck. "Where do you hurt?"

"I can't feel my foot."

"Can you wiggle your toes?"

The man shook his head.

Shelby glanced at Taylor. His face mirrored her concern. Did they share the same worry that the blood supply might be cut off to the lower part of Mr. Hartman's leg or, just as troublesome, that there a possibility he could be bleeding to death?

"John, sit with your father. I'd like to talk to

Dr. Wayne," Taylor called. The boy came closer. "We'll be right over here if you need us."

Taylor quietly pulled Shelby out of their hearing. "I'm anxious about him bleeding out without us realizing it because we won't be able to see it. I'm going to try to get a look at his leg." Taylor pulled his stethoscope off.

"How're you going to do that?" Shelby asked, her voice raised an octave.

"I'll lie on the ground and stick my hand under the bushhog and feel for his leg. If I can't do that then I'll feel on the ground for blood."

"Okay. I'll check his leg from above."

Taylor stuffed his stethoscope into his bag. Going down on his belly, he reached beneath the bush hog, searching for the man's leg. His fingertips brushed cloth that was wet and sticky. Stretching out as far as he could, he felt up and down the leg. It was bleeding but not as much as Taylor had feared.

Scooting back, he got to his feet. Shelby came to stand close beside him. "He's bleeding but not badly, considering," he said for Shelby's ears only. "The trick is to get pressure applied as soon as we can move the bush hog to prevent hemorrhage. The secondary concern is that he may lose the leg from loss of blood flow to the feet. When the ambulance does arrive, it isn't going to make it back here. We're going to have to figure out how to take him out ourselves." He looked around. "Where's that help?"

"They should be here soon." As she said the words an army of headlights came out of the woods and headed across the field.

"Thank God," Taylor whispered under his breath.

As two tractors that were part of the fire department, along with Mrs. Hartman and Jenny on the mule and several neighbors on their four-wheelers, arrived, Shelby returned to monitoring Mr. Hartman's vitals.

Taylor morphed into trauma doctor mode and began giving orders. He asked Sam to oversee the positioning of three of the four-wheelers on the other side of the ditch so that their headlights focused on the tractor and bush hog. Noise from all the engines was almost deafening in such a small area but Taylor's voice could still be heard over the din.

"John, I need you to swing your four-wheeler around to the right." The boy went running to follow Taylor's order.

A natural leader, Taylor had no trouble getting the people to respond as if they'd known and trusted him for ever.

Jenny and Mrs. Hartman appeared inside the circle of light and brought Shelby the blankets and towels. While she worked to reassure Mrs. Hartman that her husband would be fine, Taylor continued directing four-wheelers. He told two of the newly arrived drivers that he wanted them on that side of the ditch so that light would be coming from as many different angles as possible.

Shelby felt a sense of pride as she listened to Taylor organize the operation. His abilities to manage people and keep a level head in a crisis were outstanding. The man had special skills that would fit well into the community. Too bad he wasn't interested.

Rolling up a towel, she placed it under Mr. Hartman's head then covered him with a couple of blankets, tucking them in securely to hold the warmth in and slow down shock. She hoped they weren't too late to prevent it. If they couldn't get him out soon, he might die of it. He needed to be on his way to a hospital.

As the men on the tractors wrapped chains around the wrecked vehicle and attached another chain to the bush hog, Taylor instructed them on how to pull in order to minimize the damage to Mr. Hartman's leg.

Discussion broke out about the best way to perform the maneuver and Taylor interrupted the conversation, making it clear what had to be done and how otherwise Mr. Hartman could be injured further. Once again, Shelby was grateful to Taylor. Would the tough farmers have given her as much respect as they were now giving Taylor? With everything set as Taylor had ordered, and the driver of each tractor understanding his duty, Taylor approached her.

"My plan is for us to move the tractor and bush hog enough for us to assess again before we pull Mr. Hartman out. Do you agree?"

"I agree. Before the pressure is completely released we need to know how to handle it and where the bleeding is coming from. My only concern is if anything shifts when we examine him again, we might do him more harm."

"I've thought of that but I don't think we have a choice."

Shelby nodded her agreement.

She went back to Mr. Hartman. "We're getting

ready to pull you out. It shouldn't be too much longer now."

The injured man did little more than grunt.

"Okay, everybody, stand back." Taylor shouted to be heard over the roar of the tractors. Shelby moved away but not so far that she couldn't be back to the farmer's side lightning fast.

"Slowly," Taylor yelled. At tortoise speed, the tractors pulled in opposite directions. The wheel of the tractor pinning Mr. Hartman shifted. Shelby sucked in a quick breath, held it. Was Taylor's strategy going to cause more damage? Seconds later the bush hog moved slightly.

Mr. Hartman let out a moan of pain. Shelby rushed to him, going down on her knees. "Hold your positions, guys," Taylor shouted to the tractor drivers, then joined her.

"He's passed out," Shelby said.

"It'll probably be better for him this way. It's going to be painful when we lift him," Taylor said, and Shelby couldn't disagree.

"I'm going into the ditch and underneath to see what we've got before we pull him out."

"That's too dangerous." She grabbed his forearm. "Is it really necessary?"

"I think it is. I'll be fine. The tractors aren't

going anywhere. Hand me the flashlight." She did as she was told. Taylor moved to leave and she grabbed his hand. "Please be careful. I don't need you hurt too."

He squeezed her hand, then went to the edge of the ditch and sat on his butt before sliding down on it and disappearing into the gully.

"Get out of the light!" Taylor demanded from below.

She looked across the ditch to see one of the teenagers walking over to another four-wheeler.

"Hey," she hollered. "You're in the light."

The boy quickly stepped out of the way.

"That's better." Taylor's voice was muffled, telling her that he was moving farther under the tractor.

Shelby held her breath. As her imagination took hold she pictured the chains breaking, the tractor falling, Taylor being pinned underneath.

With enormous relief she watched Taylor climb out of the ditch. He came to stand beside her and offer his hand. She took it and he helped her stand.

Mrs. Hartman rushed by them to take Shelby's place beside her husband.

"We need to talk a sec." He led her out of the

ring of light, where the two of them could speak without being overheard. "He has a puncture wound high on the left thigh. A smaller one on the right. We're going to need to pull him out quickly and apply pressure immediately.

"I know how you feel about blood and I hate it that there's no other way, but you're going to need to see to the wounds and stop the bleeding."

"I'll do what has to be done."

He ran a fingertip lightly down her cheek. "That's my girl. I never doubted it."

CHAPTER EIGHT

SHELBY searched through the emergency bag until she found plastic gloves. Next she pulled out the containers of four-by-four gauze bandages and broke the paper seals. With them stacked firmly in her hand, she nodded to Taylor that she was ready. Taking a cleansing breath, she prepared herself, refusing to let him or her patient down.

Taylor reassured her with a smile then motioned the largest-looking guy over and said, "I'm going to need your help lifting Mr. Hartman. When the tractors release him, on my mark—pull. You understand?"

The man nodded and Taylor looked directly at her.

"I'm ready." Shelby stood as close to the machinery as she dared, out of Taylor's and the man's way, and waited.

Taylor put his hand in the air, waved and the tractors moved in unison and in opposite directions. He placed his hands under Mr. Hartman's armpit and low on his back, showing the large man how he wanted him to pull Mr. Hartman out. When the man matched Taylor's hands, he shouted "Pull!" Seconds later the farmer was out and Shelby was kneeling beside him, applying pressure to the bleeding wound. She ignored the roll of her stomach. She must do whatever it took to save Mr. Hartman's life. Her and Taylor's patient.

Taylor hollered, "Hold." The tractors halted as he and his helper laid Mr. Hartman on the bush hog. They adjusted their position before moving the injured man to a blanket that Jenny and her mother had placed on the ground. Across from her, Taylor remained on one knee and applied a bandage to the smaller wound, securing it.

"You got that?" He waited until she looked up.

"I'm good." Until her patient was out of her care, she had to be.

"I'm going to check for other injuries then we'll pack the wound and then splint." With efficient movements he ran his hands down Mr. Hartman's legs and up again. "Mr. Hartman, can you hear me?"

The man's groan affirmed he'd regained consciousness.

"Can you feel your toes?"

The man gave them the smallest of nods. Relief rushed through her as she returned Taylor's smile. "Great. Let's get this leg splinted and get him to a hospital," Shelby said.

"Yes, ma'am," he said in a whoosh of released breath.

He grabbed her bag, located the splints and handed one to her. Carefully and quickly they wrapped the leg, making sure the four-by-fours were securely in place.

"Jenny," she called, "pull the mule up alongside your dad." To Taylor she said, "We need to get blankets laid out on the back of the mule. This is going to be a painful ride out for him."

Taylor followed her instruction unquestioningly. Just as she'd followed his earlier. They'd switched roles, each finding their niche. She'd never experienced this type of rapport with any other doctor, not even with her husband. She and Taylor seemed to know what the other was thinking. They worked together as a smooth and skilled team.

He directed Jenny to where she needed to be and then she and Taylor saw to the padding.

"We need to keep him as level as possible," Shelby said, and turned to one of the volunteer firemen. "You brought a board, didn't you?" The lack of light made it difficult to see and she'd been too busy to search beforehand.

"Right here, Doc," one of the men called, pulling the wooden backboard towards her.

"Okay, guys, I need us to get on each side of Mr. Hartman and put our arms under him as far as you can. On three—lift."

As the men lifted, Shelby supported Mr. Hartman's head. She made a mental note to include a neck brace in her emergency bag. Once the injured man was on the mule, she and Taylor rolled towels and placed them along the man's legs and neck to stabilize them. Jenny gave them a couple of industrial straps and they used them to secure the backboard to the mule. Mrs. Hartman climbed into the passenger seat. "He's going to be fine, Mrs. Hartman."

"Okay, Jenny. Dr. Stiles and I are going to ride in back with your father. Go slowly and the fewer bumps the better." Before Shelby could finish the sentence, Taylor had lifted her up onto the mule. Their gazes met for a second. She found her seat then he went around to the other side and climbed on.

There was little space for them to sit and it wasn't going to be a comfortable ride, but it would be much worse for Mr. Hartman. As they bumped and rocked along, Taylor grabbed her arm when she threatened to fall off. A tingle went through her, then it was gone when he let go. After the third time he held her hand across the barely conscious man's chest. Mr. Hartman groaned as they went but never woke fully. She was grateful for Taylor's steadying support.

Taylor's hand was gritty and rough from the dirt caked to his fingers, but she didn't care. They were warm and reassuring around hers. His touch said he would take care of her. She liked that feeling.

The trip seemed never-ending. It was a relief to see the house lights in the distance. When they finally made it to the drive, the ambulance was waiting. As soon as Jenny stopped the mule, Taylor hopped off and came around to her to assist her in getting down. She'd been in one position for so long her legs were stiff.

"Walk around a second to ease your legs and I'll see about getting Mr. Hartman unloaded."

Shelby followed his advice and was soon able to help with getting Mr. Hartman situated in the ambulance. Mrs. Hartman gushed her thanks then climbed into the passenger seat for the ride to Nashville.

Taylor had instructed the ambulance men to take Mr. Hartman to the hospital where he himself worked, saying he'd call ahead and let them know they were coming.

"I need a phone. I left mine at home. It probably wouldn't get any service out here anyway," he said to no one in particular.

"You can use ours in the house," Jenny offered.

As the sun was coming up after a long night, Shelby watched Taylor walk towards the house. Those wide shoulders of his were solid, sure, and strong enough to lean on.

Taylor had finished his call then cleaned up in the bathroom Jenny had indicated on the way to the phone. He was headed back outside when Shelby's laughter drew him down the hallway of the old, two-story house. He liked hearing that soft ripple of sound. She didn't make it enough. Those notes led him to a huge family-style kitchen.

Shelby stood amidst volunteer firemen, tractor drivers and the kids who had been on the four-wheelers. They were all laughing and talking loudly as they filled their plates with food.

A woman Taylor had seen only briefly earlier came up beside him. "I'm Bess, a friend of the Hartmans. Mrs. Hartman told us to take care of everyone. To give you her thanks for saving her husband's life. We've prepared breakfast, so help yourself."

The group stopped talking and waved him forward to envelop him inside. Taylor hesitated before stepping forward to stand beside Shelby.

A few patted him on the back while others told him how impressed they'd been with the job he'd done. Treating him as a hero, they insisted he go first. He filled his plate with eggs, bacon and the most delicious-smelling home-made biscuits. Being accepted into a community was an alien experience but wholly wonderful.

He took a seat down at the family-style table. Shelby smiled widely as she took a seat across from him. Her eyes sparkled as she chatted with those around her. He was glad to see no visible lasting effects from Mr. Hartman's trauma. The blood hadn't prevented her from doing what had to be done. Picking up his fork, he started on his meal. He was ravenous for nourishment and for Shelby.

Shelby watched from under half-raised lids as Mr. Abernathy, a particularly boisterous, middle-aged farmer, shook Taylor's hand vigorously and invited him to go hunting. She grinned. Taylor faltered a second, before replying, "Thank you, sir. I'd like that." Taylor looked at her as if perplexed by all the camaraderie.

Shelby chuckled. When the man walked away she said to Taylor, "I guess you'll be back to hunt in the fall." That little boy who had always stood on the outside had been accepted into the fold. She just hoped he realized it.

As they ate, Taylor was peppered by questions about himself from the men and teens sitting around the table. At first he showed little enthusiasm for answering their questions but with some encouragement he became part of the crowd, even entertaining them with anecdotes.

Taylor called the hospital after finishing his meal and reported to the group that Mr. Hartman was in surgery and doing as well as expected.

Taylor received high fives all round, which he acknowledged with a grin on his face. He had a wonderful smile.

Her heart swelled with the goodness of life as she looked around the table. These people were neighbors and friends who cared about one another. They'd worked together the night before to help Mr. Hartman and now it was time to celebrate their success. Taylor was smiling broadly and he seemed much happier and more at ease with himself than he'd been when he'd first come to town. She enjoyed the opportunity to visit with everyone outside the clinic. It's a shame it took a tragedy for her to socialize more with her community. She was going to do better in the future.

Finally, knowing they'd stayed long enough, Shelby said to Taylor, "We need to go. We should've been at the clinic an hour ago."

Taylor gave her a dubious look but said his goodbyes. The others mumbled their own need to leave and followed them out. The sun had risen high enough that the area they'd traveled in the dark was clearly visible. Looking at it made her realize that she didn't want to repeat that adventure again any time soon.

When they reached the truck Taylor said he'd

drive and she'd gladly agreed, climbing into the passenger seat. "You know the way?"

"I believe I can make it," he said, as he got behind the wheel.

"Isn't it a beautiful day? I love this country." She looked at the low mountains creating the farm valley and the green fields butting up against them.

"Yes, beautiful."

Taylor's low tone filled with wonderment made her glance at him. He was looking at her. Her gaze met his and held. *He thinks I'm beautiful.* A fuzzy, pleasurable sensation trickled through her. Taylor believing that made her believe it too.

He leaned toward her, itching to kiss her, then glanced out the window at the others mingling in the yard and sat up. "Come on, Dr. Wayne. You've done a good night's work and I need to get you home."

"The clinic—"

"First things first. We both should clean up."

She rested her head against the back of the seat and closed her eyes. "We had a pretty amazing night, didn't we?" she murmured. "I guess you're used to that type of thing but I don't see it often.

Mr. Hartman was a trouper. I hope he recovers quickly. You were great, by the way."

Taylor smiled. Shelby had been on an adrenalin high and now she'd crashed. She snored softly beside him. When her head drooped, he reached over and guided it to his shoulder. A gentle sigh of acceptance blew warmly over his bare arm as she snuggled into him. Resentment for the gear-shift filled him. It didn't allow him to put his arm around her. He'd never given much thought to the benefits of a bench seat in an automobile until he'd met Shelby. He wanted her soft, warm curves next to him as much as possible.

When he pulled into the drive, Shelby roused enough to know they were home. "How come I'm so out of it and you don't seem to be tired?" she asked in a sexy, sleepy voice that made him wish to hear it every morning.

"I keep these hours way more often than you do. My body's used to it."

"I need to get it together and get to the clinic." She shook her head lightly.

"You go on and get a bath. Have a good nap and I'll handle things at the clinic this morning."

"You know, Dr. Stiles, you're starting to make

yourself indispensable," Shelby said, climbing out of the truck and walking toward her back door.

He chuckled. "I'll take that as a compliment."

Taylor hustled to his apartment and changed clothes. He'd get a bath later. He arrived at the clinic to find Carly behind the desk, fending off patients unhappy because no one had been there to see them. He saw to the patients and told Carly to start calling to reschedule appointments already on the book for that afternoon. He also asked Carly to stay until after lunch in case anyone showed up and to ask them to come back the next day. After that she could post a sign on the door to call him in case of an emergency and take the afternoon off.

A few hours later, Taylor exhaled in pleasure as he stood under the hot flow of water from the showerhead. Done, he stepped out naked into the cool of the air-conditioned room and slid beneath the sheet on his bed. The wish that Shelby lay warm and compliant next to him followed him into welcome sleep.

The thud of the door being pushed too far and the stomping of bare feet across the wooden floor snatched him from his dream. Shelby, dressed in a long T-shirt, glaring at him from above brought him fully awake.

"Why didn't you wake me? I trusted you to see to the clinic. It's after two o'clock and no one is there!"

That was his Shelby. All fire and brimstone.

He reached for her, capturing her before she could step away. With a short whoosh she landed on top of him, squirming. The smell of sleep and wild flowers tickled his nose.

"Stop wiggling, Shelby."

"Then let me go!"

"No, because I want you to listen to me."

She struggled against him. His body reacted by going to full attention. Heaven help him, he had no control around her.

"I'll listen. Just let me go," she snarled, putting her hands on either side of his head and pushing upwards. She glowered down at him.

The arching of her back brought her pelvis into more intimate contact with his swelling masculinity. "I don't think you will. Anyway, I like you right where you are." He flexed his hips.

Her eyes widened as if they had registered what she did to him. She brought her chest down to his but remained stiff against him. The only indication of her desire was her fingers curling into his shoulders. He nuzzled her neck, his lips traveling upwards to find the sweet spot behind her ear. She exhaled and turned her head slightly, giving him better access. He smiled. He had her attention now. Slowly she melted against him, purring her pleasure. He wanted her desperately, and he would have her.

Taylor moved his mouth upwards to whisper in her ear, "Listen, my little she-cat, Carly and I changed the afternoon appointments only, and she stayed until noon. I told her to take the rest of the day off and put a sign on the door to call us if there's an emergency."

He flipped her quickly onto her back, bringing his hips against her with a purposely suggestive flex. "Can you tell how much I want you, my little she-cat?" His mouth found hers.

She met him kiss for searing, slick kiss. She held his lips to hers, opening for him. All the fight and fury of earlier had been turned into red-hot passion and promise. One of her hands came up to circle his neck.

Her other hand made bold strokes over his body, exploring every dip and crevice. When her small hand pushed the sheet away and brushed over his straining manhood, he almost shattered.

Taylor pulled her hand away and captured it below his on his belly. "I'm thinking one of us has on far too many clothes."

"Mmm, and one of us has just the right amount." She placed a kiss on his shoulder and smiled as the low rumble of his chuckle vibrated beneath her.

"I believe in equality," he murmured, as his hand moved under her shirt, pushing it up and over her head. His hand found her breasts. He bestowed devotion on them that made her womb contract with escalating hunger. In short order, he saw to it that her underwear found the floor.

"Now this is fairer," he murmured as he rose over her.

Shelby waited with anticipation, acceptance and an aching desire to be his again. There was no clinic, no obligation to Benton, nothing but Taylor and how he made her feel. She pulled his lips to hers as he entered her. Once again she was his.

Later, Shelby woke to the sky turning dark blue in the east and her head supported on Taylor's firm, comfy chest. His hands were clasped possessively around her waist. She'd slept the afternoon away in Taylor's arms and she'd never felt more contented.

"Hey, there. I was starting to wonder if I needed to kiss sleeping beauty awake." Taylor's deep voice rumbled from just above her. "Not that I'd mind."

"I think that would be a rather nice way to be woken up." She lifted her face. He took her hint and his lips found hers.

A long pleasurable minute later he pulled his mouth from hers and said, "I'm hungry. How about we go out for a meal?"

"Like a date?"

He shifted onto his side and looked down at her. "Yeah, a date. The kind where I come to the front door."

She couldn't remember the last time she'd been on a date. Maybe she never had. She and her husband being childhood sweethearts had meant they had attended school and church functions together, gone to college and med school, but she couldn't remember Jim ever asking her out on a real date. They had just gone places together. She liked the idea of being thought special enough to be asked out by Taylor.

She wanted this date to be memorable. It would probably be their one and only. Despite the passionate hours they'd spent in bed, nothing had really changed. Their differences weren't about Benton. They went deeper than that. Taylor couldn't move beyond his uncertainties and memories and she couldn't leave her obligations, face her own fear of change. Taylor would go back to Nashville and she'd remain in Benton. She wanted to snatch as many happy moments she could before then. After Taylor left life would go on, but it would be sadder and lonelier.

"I don't know if the neighbors can stand you showing up at the front door again. The last time you were in your boxers."

He grinned. "This time I'll make sure to have all my clothes on."

"I rather like the red plaid number."

"Then I have to make sure to wear them again for you some time." He gave her a playful swat on the behind. "So, do you want to get a bite to eat with me or not?"

"Thank you, that sounds nice," she said primly and properly. He chuckled. Something he was doing more often these days. She'd become fond of hearing that nice, easy-rolling sound. He had a wonderful laugh, one he should use often. She'd commit it to memory and pull it out late at night. She put on a bright smile. "I'll go get ready."

He ran a hand over her bare hip. "We have a few more minutes before you need to do that."

"How did you know about this place?" Shelby asked Taylor as they were being seated at a restaurant table with a crisp white tablecloth.

"I called Mrs. Ferguson and asked her advice."

"I bet she wanted to know why you were asking."

He grinned. "She did. I told her I had a date and needed advice on somewhere special to go. She said that she thought you'd enjoy coming here."

"Once again there are no secrets in Benton." She picked up the menu.

"Did you think there would be?"

He sounded much more resigned to that idea than he'd been in the past. "I guess not. I've heard of this place but I've not had a chance to try it."

"That figures."

She pursed her lips and narrowed her eyes. Taylor reached across the table and took her hand. "I shouldn't have said that. I don't want us to fight. Let's just enjoy our meal."

After the waiter took their orders and quietly moved away, Shelby said, "I feel guilty about not going to the clinic today. That's two days in the same week. I've never done that before." She looked into his warm brown eyes. "I did enjoy my afternoon, though," she said quietly.

He gave her the smile of a man who knew he'd satisfied his woman. "Why, thank you, ma'am. I believe that's the third compliment you've ever given me. I'm honored." She longed for more afternoons like the one they'd just shared but knew there was little chance of that.

"I didn't realize a smooth-talking, fast-driving, handsome doctor from the big city needed to have his ego stroked regularly."

"I think that there's at least one more compliment in there somewhere. My, with four so close together, you really make me feel special."

"Like you don't have people telling you you're wonderful all the time. Mrs. Ferguson all but melts at your feet now."

His lids went to half-mast over his darkening eyes. "That's not the same as having you say it."

She shivered with the longing Taylor evoked in her, something only he could do. "Am I that bad?"

"Yeah, in some ways. It's been pretty hard to coerce a smile out of you at times."

She gave him a bright smile she didn't really feel. "Better?"

"Perfect." He leaned over and kissed her too slowly to be appropriate in a public place but she didn't push him away.

Their meal was outstanding and Taylor turned out to be a dream dinner companion. She wasn't surprised. Over the past couple of weeks she'd found fewer of his traits to criticize.

While they ate local catfish, she and Taylor discussed their likes and dislikes from movies to books to politics. Shelby was pleased to find that they often agreed even on their food.

The only divide between them was that he hated living in a small town, couldn't see beyond his childhood memories to appreciate the good qualities. And that gulf was Grand Canyon wide, because Benton was her haven—her place of safety and security after Jim's death. But Shelby shoved those thoughts aside. Just for this one night she wanted to enjoy being with him and not have to think of tomorrow.

They were leaving the restaurant as Roger and Mary Albright were coming in. Shelby stopped

226 HOT-SHOT DOC COMES TO TOWN

to say hello. Taylor's hand rested possessively on her waist. When she tried to step away, he pulled her more securely against him, making it clear that they were out for more than a friendly meal.

"Well, hi, Shelby," Mary simpered as her gaze fell on Taylor. "And you must be the Dr. Stiles that we've been hearing so much about."

"Taylor Stiles," he said as he nodded to Mary and shook Roger's hand. "Nice to meet you both."

"We've heard all about what happened last night from Mildred Miller. She says you were heaven sent." Mary's focus remained on Taylor.

"I don't know about that." Taylor's lips curved into a small smile. He glanced at Shelby.

More like Uncle Gene sent.

"Dr. Wayne did an excellent job also." Taylor gave her waist a squeeze.

"Well, I'm sure the Hartmans were glad you were both available," Mary said smiling in too syrupy a way for Shelby's taste.

Was Mary making a veiled reference to the fact that Taylor had turned up wearing nothing but his boxers at her front door? Shelby had no doubt that Sam had told that story more than once.

As if Taylor knew where the conversation was headed, he said, "It was a pleasure to meet you both." He nudged Shelby in the direction of the door.

"That woman's the biggest busybody in town," Shelby said when they were outside on the way to the car.

"I suspected as much," he said in a flat voice. "I'm familiar with her kind."

"I guess everyone has spent their day getting caught up on us." She resigned herself to the fact that she and Taylor would be the hot topic in the town until something new and equally titillating replaced them.

"No doubt."

She glanced at him. "You okay with that?"

"That's just how small towns are. I've accepted that the good goes with the bad. The Hartman neighbors were wonderful to us last night. When I leave I can be assured that people are looking after you. That's a good thing."

They'd reached the car and Taylor held the door open for her, so with her heart in her mouth Shelby asked him directly. "Have you learned enough to consider staying for a while longer?"

"We've already covered this subject more than once." Taylor closed the door.

They remained quiet on the ride home. Apparently her optimism that their teamwork as doctors, their compatibility in bed and the fact they'd enjoyed a nice evening together hadn't changed his mind.

He pulled into the drive and turned the car engine off, leaving them in darkness. She really should have changed the bulb in the porch when it blew yesterday.She pulled on the door latch, preparing to get out. Taylor reached across and took her hand. "Wait." The shadows falling across his face accented the serious lines.

"I had a nice time. Thank you. But I'm tired and would really just like to go in." Shelby pulled her hand away, reaching for the handle again.

"Shelby, come with me to Nashville." His voice sounded as if this was a sudden thought that he'd just blurted out. "There are plenty of practices looking for another GP as partner. You're a great doctor. You'll have no trouble finding a position."

"I can't do that."

"Yes, you can. I'll help you find someone to take over the clinic. I'll even agree to work a Saturday a month for a while."

"No. This is my home. My community depends on me. I can't just pull up and leave."

He took both of her hands in his, encouraging

her to face him. "Shelby, I realize and I think you do too, that what's between us is special. I don't want it to end. If you won't come with me then we'll just have to meet when we can. You come to Nashville or we can meet somewhere between there and here. I want to see you."

With a heavy heart she gave a shake of her head. "It would never work. Long-distance relationships are hard under the best of conditions. Our schedules alone work against us. The clinic has to be my priority."

"Above everything, and apparently everybody." His words dripped sarcasm.

"What do you mean by that?"

"The clinic is your entire life. You need to stop hanging onto that dream you had as a child. You use this town, your job as a shield against the world, being hurt. Me. It's as if you are afraid to live your life. You have to let go, for your own good. You've convinced yourself that Benton needs you when it's really you that needs Benton. You're so caught up in safeguarding yourself from any pain or loss that you can't think of anything else. Can't let go. Certainly not for me."

"Are you about through?" She pulled her hands from his.

"Not yet. You can't take care of everybody else and not take care of yourself. Before long you'll have nothing left to give to anyone. What was your dream at one time? Yours alone? I bet you can't even remember."

"You seem to have all the answers for me but what about yours? You're running from your past. You hide it behind that well-respected profession you picked. All those fine clothes and the fancy car but you still carry those little-boy scars of not being good enough."

He shook his head.

"You don't believe me? Tell me, when was the last time you spoke to anyone from your home town? When's the last time you spoke to one of your brothers? Visited them?"

"That has nothing to do with us."

"It has everything to do with us. You've come to Benton and found a place where you can belong and you don't know what to do about it. Now you're scared that you might really form lasting relationships, invest in others' lives. That terrifies you because it would mean letting go of that security blanket of bitterness you carry around.

"You even refuse to see that the people of Benton like and accept you just as you are. They haven't asked you to prove yourself. What you can't see is that you're the one not accepting them." She waved trembling hands.

"Look what you have accomplished," she continued, her voice no longer gentle. "You're a doctor. And a darned good one. You've come to town and made friends. People like you. Here you could make a real difference. Here you've found that acceptance you've searched so hard for but you push it away."

Angry words hung heavily between them before Taylor asked in a tight voice, "Are you done? I see that you didn't have the same trouble with the psych rotation that you did with emergency."

Despite being unable to see his face well, Shelby had no doubt that his jaw was clenched piano-string tight. She'd hurt his feelings. Something she'd not intended to do. Still, she'd said things he'd needed to hear. She reached for him. "Taylor—"

"Look, I think we should just call it a night," he said, sliding out of the car.

She was already out and closing the door by the time he'd made it around to help her. If she didn't hurry inside she'd break down in front of him. Something she fought against doing.

He didn't touch her on the way to her door and they didn't speak. Taylor waited at the bottom of the steps, making no move to stop her from going in. She closed the door with a finality that made her heart break. She watched out the window through watery eyes as Taylor slowly climbed the stairs to the apartment.

How was she going to survive the next two days with him so near and them miles apart at the same time?

CHAPTER NINE

SHELBY arrived at the clinic earlier than usual on Saturday morning. She might as well be there as in her bed, willing her mind and body to stop thinking about Taylor. Her plan was to get some work done but that wasn't happening. She understood loss, had experienced it acutely, but Taylor's departure today was a deeper pain than she'd ever known.

Pushing the folders on the desk away, she crossed her arms, laid her head on them and closed her eyes. The stiffness in her shoulders remained no matter how often she'd rolled them, searching for relief. Taking a deep breath, she released it gradually, hoping the oxygen would clear her mind. Nothing could ease the despair that the next few hours would bring.

She'd feared this would happen. This horrible suffering was the reason she'd worked to keep Taylor uninvolved in her life. But it hadn't worked. He'd found a stronghold in her heart.

She should've protected herself better. She would from now on.

Taking another deep breath and releasing it, she said, "Keep the connection friendly. Don't start to care. Do whatever it takes to survive."

Yesterday she'd given serious consideration to calling her uncle and bragging about Taylor, encouraging the judge to give him a day and a half's amnesty. That would at least allow the pain to be quick and sharp instead of the lingering ache she now carried. She hadn't called but only because she hadn't been able to stand the thought of Taylor leaving any sooner than scheduled. That made no sense. She'd become irrational. Her emotions were all over the place.

She and Taylor had made it through the workday Friday with little interaction. Because the clinic had been closed the afternoon before, they'd had little time to eat lunch, much less talk. Still her desire for him had simmered, threatening to burst into flame if he'd given her even the slightest touch.

She'd stayed in her office doing paperwork until her normal departure time. Hidden out, if she admitted the truth, until Taylor had left. He'd said a polite goodnight as she'd locked the door for the day. When she'd left, she'd gone to the grocery store for some much-needed staples and dog food, not trusting herself not to run into Taylor at home. She had decided to keep Buster. With a living and breathing thing around when she came home, it wasn't nearly as lonely.

To cheer herself up, she decided a haircut was in order. Plus, it would keep her away from the house until bedtime. Taylor had managed to stop her from going to her own home. Her haven. She'd become fragile where he was concerned. Her greatest fear was that she'd climb the stairs to the apartment and ask him to take her into his arms.

Enough of those thoughts. Sitting up, she pushed her clinic office chair back and went to the restroom. She studied her face in the mirror. Her eyes were bloodshot from crying and no rest. She couldn't show up looking like this to Mrs. Ferguson's tea. Turning on the cold water, she let it run until it was ice cold before splashing it in her face.

As she patted her cheeks dry, footsteps approached in the hall. She'd know those anywhere. Taylor. Pushing her hair back into place, she took a deep breath.

Opening the door, she found him propped against the wall, his head down, shoulders slumped. His head rose. He gave her a direct look, studying her. That warmth that smoldered within her any time he came near began to bubble. The disks of darkness under both his eyes testified to the fact he'd not been sleeping any better than she had.

Her fingers spasmed with the need to pull him to her and make all that misery disappear. If she allowed that one show of weakness, she wouldn't be able to stop herself from begging him to stay. That she couldn't do. He had to want to be here or they'd never find happiness. Above all, she wished for him to be happy. Even if it wasn't with her.

"Shelby," he said longingly, as he straightened and stepped toward her.

She put a hand out, stopping his advance while being careful not to make physical contact. "Please don't." The need to feel sheltered in his embrace warred with her need to protect her heart from further pain.

"I'm sorry for those things I said," he said gently.

"I'm sorry for what I said too. How you live isn't my business."

He flinched but recovered quickly. "Can't we just start over?" his chocolatey eyes pleaded. "At least be friends."

"We are friends." With a firm resolve that Shelby would've never guessed she possessed, she said, "I think that's all it can ever be between us." She couldn't keep the melancholy out of her voice.

Taylor stepped toward her. She moved away, meeting the wall behind her. He didn't touch her but he stood close enough that she smelled the citrus of his shaving cream and the scent she knew so well. She took a deep breath, committing that aroma to memory.

"I don't want to go with this…uh…" he searched for the right word "…thing between us," he finished.

"Look, we just want different things. I can't leave and you can't stay. It's as simple as that." But saying the words made her realize that it was so much more.

"You make it sound so final."

"Taylor, you've never led me to believe anything but that you'd be gone after your time here was over. You've been nothing but honest, so you have nothing to feel guilty about."

He moved nearer but didn't touch her. Close enough that if she inhaled deeply her breasts would brush his chest. "Come on, Shelby," he whispered in a raspy voice. "Reconsider my offer. We're so good together."

"I can't."

"Why?"

"Because I want things you can't give me."

"Like?" His breath brushed across her cheek.

Her gaze met his piercing one. "I want to work here, live here, raise a family here."

"Does it have to be all or nothing?"

"For me it does."

His hand gently cupped her cheek. "I'm sorry you feel that way. We could be so good together." His fingers caressed her skin before they fell away.

Taylor's words rang in her ears as he walked toward the front of the building.

At noon, Taylor logged out of Shelby's computer for the last time and pushed the chair back from the desk. Massaging his neck with his hands, he prepared himself for the next few hours. He had to return to Shelby's apartment and pack then attend Mrs. Ferguson's birthday tea. After that, he'd put Benton in his rearview mirror for good.

He'd already checked in with the hospital and learned he was scheduled to work the next morning at seven. He was pleased with that information because he was ready to return to the busy emergency room. There he would just practice medicine, not get involved in people's lives.

"Uncle Gene" would expect him to appear in court in the next day or so. Taylor was sure the judge would be calling Shelby for a report on how he'd done during the last two weeks. Would she let on to Uncle Gene that they had become more than colleagues? He didn't think so. He was completely confident that what happened between him and Shelby on a personal level wouldn't help his cause with the judge.

Taylor checked his watch. There was just enough time to pick up his dress shirt from the cleaners, get back to the apartment, shower and change, and pack before party time. He'd asked Carly for directions to the church, planning to leave town directly from there. He didn't even try to ask Shelby if she'd like to ride to the party with him. He already knew what her answer would be.

An hour and a half later, he came down the

stairs with his bag over his shoulder. Shelby's truck was sitting out on the street. She must be inside, getting ready to attend the tea. The temptation to knock on her back door was only prevented by his better judgment. Hadn't they already said everything they needed to say?

Taylor opened the trunk of his car and tossed his bag in with more force than necessary. He stayed seated behind the wheel of the car for a moment before starting it and backing out of the drive. He'd never be required to come back here again. Mr. Marshall, the neighbor across the street, smiled and waved from his mailbox. Taylor returned the greeting then glanced at Shelby's house. What was he hoping? That she'd be looking out the window for a glimpse of him? His heart said he was leaving more than an unmade bed on this tree-lined street.

Minutes later he pulled into the parking lot of a small white clapboard church with a red-brick addition on the back. There were few cars in the lot. He'd made a point of coming early so he could be on his way back to Nashville before it got too late. He followed what looked like a family walking in the direction of the annexe. One of them carried a beautifully wrapped present.

Heck, he'd forgotten all about a gift. He'd just have to send one later. Maybe flowers.

He bet Shelby liked flowers. Were daisies her favorite or roses? Those thoughts were taking him nowhere.

He adjusted his tie. The irony that he had come full circle didn't escape him. He'd not worn these clothes since he'd arrived in town. Each day he'd become more casual in his choice of clothing. That morning he'd dressed in a T-shirt and cargo shorts to work the few hours at the clinic. Now he was back in his city clothes. He pulled at his collar.

Entering the fellowship hall, he was greeted with smiles by a couple of patients he recognized. Mrs. Ferguson, sitting in a wing-back chair at the end of the rectangular room, holding court. Children surrounded her dressed in what had to be their Sunday finest. They must be her grandchildren.

A young woman wearing a bright blue dress with large pink flowers on it approached him. "You must be Dr. Stiles. By my mother's description, I'd know you anywhere. She has nothing but high praise for you. I'm so glad you came."

Taylor smiled. Mrs. Ferguson's daughter might

not look a great deal like her but she certainly had the old woman's personality. "Yes, I'm Taylor Stiles. Thank you for inviting me."

"Do help yourself to some food and tea." She indicated a long table covered in a white cloth across the room.

"Thank you, I will. But I'd like to speak to your mother first."

"She'll be glad to see you. She's so disappointed you're leaving."

He nodded, grateful that a couple entering the room caught the woman's attention.

Mrs. Ferguson smiled brightly as he approached and made an effort to stand. "Please don't get up," he said, taking longer strides to get there before she could rise. "It's your birthday and you have the right to act like a queen today."

The woman giggled, her heavy jowls swinging. "I'm so happy you came."

"I wouldn't have missed it." He took her hand and grinned down at her. He liked the old bird. He would miss her.

"I can't talk you into staying with us? I'm sure Dr. Wayne would love to have your help."

"Dr. Stiles has a job and a life in Nashville. We can't expect him to just give that up."

He turned but hadn't needed to in order to know Shelby stood there. He heard the voice in his dreams, remembering her cries of pleasure as she reached her peak.

She wore a dress tucked and darted in all the correct places to accent the curves of her slim figure. The pale peach color complemented her complexion perfectly. Her shapely legs were showcased to their best advantage by the knee-length hem and her small feet were adorned by a pair of silver sandals.

She'd pulled her hair away from her face on one side, giving her a sophisticated look. There was a hint of pink on her lips that made him want to kiss it away. Shelby took his breath. She was a shining jewel in a room of uncut stones.

"I guess we can't ask him to completely change his life," Mrs. Ferguson said in a voice that implied she wasn't convinced.

What? Taylor was so utterly captivated by Shelby that he'd forgotten what they'd been discussing. His gaze met Shelby's for a second before she looked at Mrs. Ferguson. Her eyes held a sad but resigned look.

"Happy birthday, Mrs. Ferguson." Shelby offered a present wrapped in bright red paper. "This is from Dr. Stiles and me."

Taylor had to work to keep his surprise from showing.

"Honey, you two shouldn't have, but I do love presents."

One of the little girls playing nearby got up and came over. The child started tugging the corners of the paper off the present. "This is my fifth grandbaby, Audrey," she said, glancing up at Taylor and Shelby. "Would you like to help me open it, sugar pie?" she asked the girl. She nodded and went at the present in earnest.

Minutes later Mrs. Ferguson lifted out a floral print scarf that she promptly wrapped about her neck. "I love it. Thank you both." She smiled her pleasure.

"You're very welcome," Taylor said. "It looks wonderful on you." The woman beamed. "Dr. Wayne has good taste."

"It's does look perfect on you," Shelby said.

When another guest drew near he said, "I think I'll take Dr. Wayne over for a bite to eat. Again, happy birthday."

He cupped Shelby's elbow, counting on her not making a scene.

"Happy birthday," Shelby said, before Taylor ushered her away.

"Thank you for including me in on the present. I'd not thought to get one and was going to send her some flowers tomorrow."

"You're welcome," Shelby said, without looking at him.

He let his hand drop when she moved far enough away that he could no longer cradle her elbow.

Shelby balanced her plate on her lap as she took a sip of tea. Taylor sank onto a chair next to hers. They ate silently, as if they were strangers. She missed that simple camaraderie they'd shared so many times, longed for it again. Grief filled her for what they'd so briefly shared and lost. She cared too much for Taylor for them not to at least part as friends.

"Taylor, I'm sorry about…uh…things."

"I am too. Will you walk me out to the car?"

She wasn't sure it would make a difference in the long run but she couldn't say no. "I guess so. We just need to stay long enough not to be rude."

A few minutes later Taylor took her plate and cup. "It's time I headed out," he said. He stood, walked over to where the dirty dishes were being gathered and placed theirs with the rest.

Her gaze followed him as he moved away in his self-assured, loose-hipped stride. He was too handsome for words. Dressed in a light blue shirt and striped tie that was no doubt silk, he sported the air of a suave and confident male. His navy slacks fit his trim hips and molded to his behind perfectly. They were supported by a thin brown belt. She smiled as she remembered the day he'd arrived. Taylor had been wearing those same shoes.

Shelby committed everything about him to memory so she could bring them out in the blackest part of the night.

As Taylor walked back to her, he smiled. This one reached his eyes. Her heartbeat did a clip-clop. She couldn't help but return it.

"Ready?" he asked, offering his hand.

"Shouldn't we say goodbye to Mrs. Ferguson?"

He glanced over at her. A group of people surrounded her. "I don't think she'll miss us."

Shelby placed her hand in his. It felt right to touch him. She let Taylor help her stand. As soon as she did, she pulled her fingers from his. Letting herself hope would only make it hurt more.

They'd reached the door when "Oh"s and "Help"s rang out. She turned. Mrs. Ferguson was slumped in her chair.

"Taylor..." She grabbed his forearm for a second before they hurried to Mrs. Ferguson.

"Someone call nine-one-one," Shelby called.

"Move back," Taylor snapped in an authoritative voice that made those surrounding the limp woman react. Even the children quit playing. There was no clink of utensils on plates or sounds of laughter. Everyone was focused on Mrs. Ferguson.

Reaching the woman, Taylor went down on a knee and brushed her hair away from her face. "Mrs. Ferguson, can you hear me?" Getting no response, he said, "Help me get her on the floor."

With the help of three other men Taylor maneuvered the large woman out of the chair, cradling her head so that it wouldn't hit the floor. Her eyes remained closed. She was deathly pale and her lips were a dusky blue.

Shelby went down on her knees and placed two fingers on Mrs. Ferguson's neck to check for a pulse in her carotid artery. Taylor came down beside her.

"No pulse. We'll have to start CPR."

She checked the airway for obstructions. "I'll handle the airway. You do compressions."

Taylor removed his tie with two quick jerks and threw it to the floor. He then located the correct spot on Mrs. Ferguson's breastbone to push. Stacking his hands one on top of the other, straightening his arms and locking his elbows, he began to push down on Mrs. Ferguson's chest.

The only sound in the room was Taylor's calm but firm voice counting, "Twenty-seven, twenty-eight, twenty-nine, breath." That was her cue to lean over and give Mrs. Ferguson two breaths. Taylor continued, "One, two, three…"

Sweat popped out on his brow but she couldn't take the time to wipe it away. For what felt like an age they worked in tandem to save Mrs. Ferguson's life.

The puff of breath from Mrs. Ferguson touched Shelby's face as she went down to breathe. She sat up. Mrs. Ferguson's eyelids fluttered. Taylor must have seen it too because he stopped compressions. The woman's eyes opened, closed and opened again.

"Mrs. Ferguson, nice to see you back." Taylor gave the woman a weak smile but sounded much more composed than Shelby felt. "Don't move. An ambulance is on the way."

Standing, he dug into his pocket and brought out his keys. Tossing them to the man nearest him, he said, "Get my bag out of my car, front seat. Red sports car."

The man hustled away.

"Don't try to speak," Shelby instructed as she picked up Mrs. Ferguson's wrist and began checking her pulse.

The man returned with the medical bag. Taylor pulled out his stethoscope and listened to their patient's chest. Done, he stuffed the instrument back into the bag. "Heartbeat's strong but not as steady as I'd like," he told Shelby.

With great relief she saw the private ambulance personnel enter the building with a gurney in tow. Not for the first time she wished the area could afford EMTs to staff the transportation but that just wasn't possible.

Mrs. Ferguson opened her eyes and looked at Taylor. "Doctor?" Her voice quivered.

Taylor took her hand. "Don't talk. You're going to be just fine." His voice was low and sweet with concern, which told Shelby he'd come to care for the feisty woman. As the ambulance personnel worked to prepare her for transport, he continued to hold Mrs. Ferguson's hand.

Without releasing her, he'd managed to pull his phone out of his pants pocket. He punched one number and gave a succinct report and rapid-fire instructions that assured his directions would be followed. He'd arranged for a cardiologist to be standing by in Trauma when Mrs. Ferguson arrived at the hospital.

Shelby continued to monitor the woman's vital signs as the ambulance personnel worked with the help of Taylor and a number of men to lift Mrs. Ferguson onto the gurney and then into the ambulance.

"I'm riding with her," Taylor announced in a tone that dared anyone to argue with him. He climbed into the vehicle without a backward look. The doors closed with a slam of finality before the ambulance roared off, siren blaring.

Shelby stood mountain still, staring at the back of the emergency vehicle as it pulled onto the highway. A lump of finality became thick in her middle. Her heart squeezed tight in anguish. Blinking twice, three times, she tried to prevent moisture from forming in her eyes. Everything in her wanted to scream *Come back* but that wouldn't happen. Taylor was gone.

As Taylor left Benton in the back of the ambulance headed for Nashville, he made the decision not to return. He'd convinced himself that it was best for Shelby if he sent someone for his car and belongings. The truth was that he was a coward. He couldn't look into her gray eyes that compelled him to stay and say goodbye.

Mrs. Ferguson made it to the hospital without further issues but had to have surgery for two blocked arteries. She came through the operation well and recovered nicely. The only glitch, as she put it, was the rigid diet and lifestyle changes she had to agree to. The feisty old girl would make it hard on her cardiologist but she'd do as she was instructed. This time she'd been lucky.

Taylor visited her daily and spoke to her cardiologist regularly. He'd been informed by the attending doctor that Shelby had called a number of times to check on the patient. Everything in Taylor wished he'd been the one to pick up the phone when she'd been on the line. He yearned to hear her voice. When the time came for Mrs.

Ferguson to be released from the hospital, Taylor was there to wheel her out.

"You need to think about where you belong, young man," Mrs. Ferguson told him firmly as he helped her into her daughter's car.

On their ride to Nashville he would've argued that it was right here, being a trauma doctor. But now...

Taylor had been confident that he'd return to his position in the emergency department as if he'd never been gone. A couple of shifts later he'd recognized he was taking more time with his patients than he'd done before, listening more carefully to their needs. The nurses had looked at him oddly when he'd requested to speak to the family of one of his patients.

One of his colleagues had asked, "Taylor, what're you doing, talking to the family? You never did that before."

"The family deserves to hear how their loved one is doing straight from the doctor. Rules can sometimes be more in the interest of the hospital than the needs of the patient and their family."

A week after his return his superior pulled him aside. "I hear you're taking time to speak to the families. As commendable as that is, I understand that it's causing a backlog on your shift. Especially on the busy nights."

"Maybe so, but I think it's important."

"In this hospital that job falls to the social workers. You need to let them do their jobs."

Taylor nodded in understanding but not in agreement. If he had to pick a point where his disillusionment with working in a large hospital began, it was then. He was no longer satisfied with caring for patients and passing them off to another doctor. Taylor wanted to follow up his patients, see their progress, continue to care for them, build relationships with them. To his shock, he sought what he'd had in Benton.

His time outside away from the hospital didn't ease his discontent with his life choices either. He missed looking out the window and being able to see the stars at night. Living in the center of a large city, the glow of lights all night didn't allow for stargazing. Regularly enjoying the sun rising over the tops of trees was out of the question also.

He'd lived on the seventh floor of a high-rise apartment building for the last three years and he still didn't know his neighbors. In less than a week he'd met everyone on Shelby's street and could call them by name. He would've never imagined something like that would've mattered to him.

More than anything, he missed Shelby. Thoughts of her were as continuous as a movie replaying over and over. Her smile, her eyes, her laugh, her touch…

Often, when he cared for a patient, he'd wonder what Shelby would say about this. How would she handle this situation? Would she do this differently? At work, at home or at social gatherings thoughts of her intruded. More than that he missed their sparring, her intellect, her soft heart. With Shelby could he have a solid relationship? Did he love her enough to try?

He'd made an effort to continue where he'd left off with his social life but it seemed dull and uninteresting after being around Shelby. She and Benton had so infiltrated his life that nothing in his old existence satisfied him any more. He missed the belonging and acceptance that he'd searched for his entire life and found in Benton. Now he wanted it back. How had the small town and a petite firecracker of a woman managed to change him so quickly, so totally?

If he had any hope of Shelby accepting him

as more than a partner in the clinic, as her partner for a lifetime, he had to face the demons
in his past.

CHAPTER TEN

SHELBY opened the clinic at the same time she had every workday for years. The one exception was that she didn't have the same enthusiasm she ordinarily did at the thought of a new day. The sun had risen big and bright and all she could think about was how much she'd love to spend the day taking pictures. Maybe sit in the back-yard swing and sip lemonade.

She was going to start taking some time off.

Taylor had been gone for six weeks and the truth of what he'd said was ringing true. She should train the community to see her during the hours she was open. An emergency number would always be posted if she was needed. Wednesdays were usually slow. If she took those afternoons then she'd have most of the week covered.

She'd try it starting next week. That way the word could get out. With a plan in place she went about preparing for the day with a little more spring in her step.

Flipping the computer on, she quickly checked her emails. The name Dr. Mark Singer caught her attention. Tapping a key, she opened the email and scanned the text. Dr. Singer wrote that he was interested in interviewing for a position at the clinic. He'd like her to contact him as soon as possible. Shelby's fingers flew over the keyboard as she shot off a reply. She couldn't replace Taylor in her heart but maybe she could find someone to measure up in patient care. But even that was going to be difficult.

Taylor had been gone only a few weeks but she felt his loss at the clinic daily. She'd not realized how much her workload had consumed her life until he'd been there. Weeks later the patients were still asking about Taylor, wanting to know if she had heard from him.

There were reminders of him everywhere at the clinic, in the apartment, in her kitchen, and more painfully in her heart. Since he'd left with Mrs. Ferguson he'd not called. It hurt. Terribly.

She'd seen to it that his car had been driven to her house from the church. A couple of days later she had been both surprised and offended when a uniformed stranger had shown up at the clinic.

"I'm here to pick up..." the man had looked at a paper "...a Taylor Stiles's car. I was given this address." He'd looked around as if unsure he'd been in the correct place.

"May I see that?" Shelby's hand had shaken slightly as she'd taken the official-looking sheet. Taylor's bold signature had appeared on the line in the bottom right-hand corner. She knew it well. He hadn't even bothered to come and get his car. Was he done with anything that had to do with Benton, including her?

Shelby had instructed the man to follow her home. She'd stood in the drive and watched as he'd driven away in the car. It had been the final, indisputable statement that Taylor wasn't returning.

She phoned the hospital daily to get a report on Mrs. Ferguson's progress but never spoke to Taylor. She'd not really anticipated she would. The cardiology service was in charge of Mrs. Ferguson's care now. That knowledge still didn't stop her heart from beating faster as she waited for the doctor to answer the phone or prevent the disappointment she felt when the voice on the other end wasn't Taylor's deep, sexy one.

After Carly arrived at the clinic, they went to work seeing patients. By lunchtime Shelby was ready to get off her feet. She dropped into the chair behind her desk. Selecting the correct key on the computer keyboard, she brought up her emails. There was a reply from Dr. Singer. He and his wife were going to be in the Benton area that afternoon and wondered if they might stop in and see the clinic.

Overwhelmed at the possibility of finding someone to help her at long last, she quickly responded with her phone number and that she'd love to meet him and his wife. With the idea of impressing the doctor, Shelby hustled around and saw that everything was neat and tidy in the clinic before she left for lunch.

An hour later she sat at her kitchen table, having a sandwich with her phone nearby. She pulled towards her the pile of mail she'd gotten out of the mailbox when she'd arrived home. Releasing the rubber band, she found the photography periodical she subscribed to encircling the rest of her mail. She pushed the envelopes aside and straightened out the bent magazine. Six months' worth of the same reading material was stacked on the footstool in the living room. She'd not had time to open even one of them in a long time.

That was another change she was going to make. Taking a bite out of her sandwich, she explored the glossy pages of the magazine. A photo contest advertisement caught her attention. It called for pictures taken in the outdoors. All entries would receive a critique and the winner would have a showing of their work. The pictures that she'd taken at the old house certainly met the criteria. This would be a good opportunity to receive some easy feedback on her photography and a chance to move forward towards doing more with her hobby. The due date was soon. The pictures needed to be sent in right away. This would be her first step out into the world. She'd do it.

As she took her plate to the sink, the phone rang. Setting the plate down, she hurried back to answer the call. Dr. Singer was on the line and said that he was driving into town. Shelby gave him directions to the clinic, ended the conversation and snatched up her keys. Maybe the doctor would be the solution to at least one of her problems. Only time could heal how she felt about Taylor.

"So, Dr. Singer, do you think you might be interested in working with me?" Shelby asked an hour later.

"I think this just might be the right place for me," the silver-haired man said. "What do you think, Betty?" He looked at his smiling wife.

"For a supposedly retired doctor who won't give medicine up completely, I think it would be ideal. But no more than a couple of days a week. I'll need help with our dream home."

At Shelby's questioning look, Dr. Singer said, "We heard about the lake and thought it would be a nice place to build. We'll look for a place to rent until we can buy the right lot. Hopefully I can start work in about a week."

"That sounds absolutely wonderful," Shelby said, with her first true smile since Taylor had left.

Having Dr. Singer's help wouldn't entirely solve her staffing problem at the clinic but it was a step in the right direction. No matter how good a physician Dr. Singer was, he couldn't replace Taylor. Certainly not in her heart. No one could substitute for Taylor there. It was wonderful to have the requirements of the clinic being met but what about her needs? Only Taylor could give her that. The clinic's issues were resolving while hers had intensified to an unrelenting ache in her heart.

Taylor had been right. The clinic was more than a two-person operation but having another doctor would at least satisfy the state's concerns. She'd still need to look for additional help but there was a sense of relief and release knowing now she could occasionally get away from the clinic. She was already planning how to spend her extra time off.

Maybe she would go to Nashville. She recognized Taylor had been right when she'd gotten over being mad and thought about it. She had been using her job and Benton to protect her from further unhappiness. Staying in Benton was safe for her, familiar. It offered her a haven that meant she didn't have to risk herself, her heart. It was easy to stay there and not have any conflict. Keeping Taylor at arm's length had done the same thing but it wasn't living. She refused to let any time she could spend with Taylor disappear because she was too scared to grasp it.

Was it too late to contact Taylor? She'd wanted to call him hundreds of times. Pride had stopped her. But pride was a cold and lonely bed companion in the middle of the night. Would Taylor still want her? Had he moved on?

She'd never know unless she took the chance to find out. He'd asked her to meet him halfway and she'd refused. If she wanted Taylor, she was going to have to tell him. If they both desired a relationship badly enough, they could work something out. Snatching some time here and there was better than nothing. Better than thinking about him day and night, and carrying around heartache that seemed to never ease.

Decision made. Next Wednesday, she was going to Nashville to see if Taylor was still willing to find that compromise he'd pleaded with her to consider. She hoped with all her heart he still wanted her.

Taylor slowed his car as he entered the city limits of the town he'd grown up in. His stomach knotted but he kept going. He'd not crossed this particular line since he'd been eighteen years old and that had been on his way out of town. If he'd been a betting man, he wouldn't have put money on him ever returning. He huffed. He would've lost.

As with a number of things he'd done in the last

couple of months, he would've sworn it would never happen. He'd amazed himself more than once.

He'd looked on the internet for his brothers' addresses. He wasn't even sure they were still living here. There were a number of Stileses living in the area. Both brothers had such common first names that the list of possibilities was great so he'd decided to drive there, then ask around. Before going to the police station for help, he wanted to see if anything had changed. If any of the bad memories had dimmed.

Circling the stately red-brick courthouse with the white dome that still commanded the square in the heart of town, Taylor found that much about it remained the same. The stores surrounding the county building were the same type that had been there years earlier with a few new ones here and there. People mingled on the sidewalks, talking or going in and out of businesses. Nothing seemed as horrifying or uncaring as he remembered. It could have been Benton's twin town.

Astonished that he felt no animosity but curiosity instead, he turned right out of town, driving past the high school. It appeared no different than he remembered from the outside. Was there a kid in there having to fight every day to survive?

Continuing on for another mile, he made a right beside the rustic general store where old man Carr had given him those words of encouragement. He smirked. Even now there were a couple of men sitting there, talking. Nothing had changed.

The road took him out of the populated area to where the houses were spaced farther apart. As he traveled, his stomach constricted. Hadn't he buried all those ugly feelings about his father long ago? All he had to do was ride down this road to have them resurface. He went round the bend in the road and slowed to a crawl. The house he was looking for stood on the right, or at least the one he thought he was looking for. This one was nothing like he remembered.

The tiny clapboard house was painted a pristine white. The porch had large ferns hanging along the front of the porch. There was now a white picket fence surrounding the yard and late-summer flowers were blooming in the beds on either side of the wide limestone stone steps leading to the door.

Taylor would've sworn that this wasn't the boyhood home where he'd spent eighteen miserable years. It was the same house, but then again it wasn't. Now it looked like a place where a happy family lived.

A man came out the door and walked towards a truck parked on the white rock drive. A jolt of disbelief rocked through Taylor.

Matt. He looked different than Taylor remembered him but still it was his older brother. Why was he here?

Taylor pulled off onto the shoulder of the road. Taking a deep breath, he climbed out of his car. The man looked at him questioningly. Then a surprised look came over his face.

"Taylor? Is that you?"

"Hello, Matt," Taylor said flatly.

Matt came toward him and Taylor moved to meet him. "I never expected to see you again."

"And I never expected to come here again."

Matt offered his hand. Accepting it, Taylor shook it then was pulled into Matt's hug. Taylor's body tensed for a second then he returned the hug. His animosity wasn't towards his brother. He'd endured living with his father just as he himself had.

"It's so good to see you," Matt said. "Please

come in. My wife and children should be back soon. I'd love you to meet them."

Taylor looked at the house, and hesitated.

"Why don't we sit on the front porch for a while?" Matt suggested.

Taylor nodded his agreement.

As they walk toward the house his brother said, "I've kept up with you, you know."

The astonishment Taylor felt must have shown on his face.

His brother grinned. "The internet makes the world a small place. I tell everyone from the old days that you became a doctor. From what I read, a good one."

They each took one of the two rockers on the porch.

"So what brought you here?" Matt asked.

"Actually, I came to see if I could find you and Bud. But I didn't think it would be so easy."

"Bud isn't in town. He's in the state pen for armed robbery. He's not due out for another five years," Matt said matter-of-factly. "I tried to help him but he was too much like Dad to listen."

Taylor felt nothing one way or the other about his brother being incarcerated. Truthfully, he was surprised he wasn't dead. The life Bud had been living when Taylor had left town had led to nothing but destruction. He'd had to deal with men like his brother during almost every night shift he'd ever worked.

"How did you come to be living here?" Taylor asked, wonder filling his voice.

"I was on the same road as Dad and Bud." His brother spoke as if he was looking into the dark past and not liking what he saw. Taylor knew well how they had been. His older brothers had been coming in drunk and high by the time Taylor had been in middle school.

"I was in and out of trouble with the law and the same with jobs until my wife came into my life. If I wanted her, I had to make a change. A major change in my life. I did and I'm a better man for it. We now have two kids. A boy and a girl. Our family..." he pointed between himself and Taylor "...wasn't pretty, no place to see an example, and I still have to work daily to beat my addiction, but life is good. We all have a past and I just choose not to let mine control me."

That was what Taylor had let his do to him and still did. Shelby had pointed that out loud and clear. If it hadn't been for her, he wouldn't be here today.

Matt lived in the same town he'd grown up in and he had been able to put his past behind him. Taylor had run away and guilded it in fast cars, society women and an expensive lifestyle. Truthfully, his brother seemed to have done a better job of dealing with his past than he had.

They rocked in silence for a while. "Why live here?" Taylor blurted. "This house?"

"Because I thought I could replace so many of my ugly memories with happy ones if I raised my family here. I could try to make this house have what Mother wanted it to have. A family who loved each other. Do you have a wife? Any children?" Matt asked.

"No."

"A good woman can change your life."

That Taylor already knew. He should take a lesson from his brother. They'd taken different roads when they'd left home but each had needed to overcome their shared past. Matt seemed to have done so, now it was his own turn.

If he hadn't hurt Shelby so badly that she no longer wanted him.

Shelby agreed to take pictures at Mrs. Ferguson's postponed birthday tea turned welcome-home party. Word had gotten out about Shelby's skills at photography when the local weekly paper was contacted about her being a finalist in the photo contest she'd entered.

After Mrs. Ferguson returned home from the hospital, she visited the clinic to let Shelby check her over. The woman begged Shelby to take pictures at the party despite her insisting she wasn't that type of photographer. Mrs. Ferguson wouldn't take no for an answer. Giving in, Shelby decided she might as well make the most of the opportunity to add to her portfolio.

The party was winding down now, and for that Shelby was grateful. On her feet most of the day, all she could think about was propping them up, watching a good movie on TV and having Buster sit on her lap. She loved the little dog dearly, though he was a bitter-sweet reminder of Taylor.

"Dr. Stiles," someone said.

Shelby went stock still. It couldn't be.

"Hello, Mrs. Ferguson, you look wonderful."

Shelby's heart went to her throat. *Taylor.* She'd recognize that voice anywhere, even in a crowd. With her back to the door, she'd not seen him enter.

She turned. Her eyes feasted on him. He was

everything she remembered and more. Charming smile, dark hair, and too handsome for words. He wore a knit shirt, tan slacks and loafers. There was a relaxed appearance about him that hadn't been there the first time he'd come to town.

Her chest ached, reminding her to breath.

What was he doing here? Had he come to town just for this party? Was there some other reason he was here? Dared she hope?

Giving herself a mental shake, she brought her camera up to her face. She struggled to steady her hands as she clicked the shutter. After all, picture-taking was what she was here for, not to gape at the people who attended. Continuously snapping pictures, she rotated to get the last of the attendees.

"Hi, Shelby."

Act cool. Don't let him see that he rattles you. "Hello, Taylor. I'm surprised to see you here."

"I figured you might be."

"What brought you back? Were you caught speeding again?" She couldn't keep the bite out of the question.

He smiled. "I was. I threw myself on the mercy of the court and asked your Uncle Gene to sentence me to Benton again."

She lowered the camera. "You are kidding, aren't you?"

"Yeah, sort of."

"What does that mean?"

He looked around the almost empty room. "You done here? I'd rather not have my driving record discussed around town if I can help it."

Nothing was secret in this town.

"I'll have to let Mrs. Ferguson know I'm leaving."

She had no idea what was going on in Taylor's mind. What she did know was that until she knew what he was doing here she wasn't going to let him hurt her again. She'd only barely managed to stop thinking about him all day long. The nights were still out of her control. Taylor dropping in for a friendly visit would be enough to tip the balance.

He waited at the door and joined her as she stepped out into the evening breeze. When her lightweight flowing silk dress threatened to blow upwards she hurriedly pushed it down.

"You know, you're the most beautiful creature." The awe in his voice made her look at him. "I've missed you. The hardest thing I've ever done was to stay away."

"Please don't…" She couldn't listen to those kinds of words from him. She so desperately wanted them to be true. Another gust of wind caught her dress. Her camera case slipped off her shoulder as she reached down to hold her dress in place.

Taylor took the bag from her and looked around the parking lot. "Where's your truck?"

"Darn, I forgot. It's in the shop. Sam had to give me a ride."

"That Sam sure is a handy guy to have around." The sarcasm in his voice didn't escape her but she didn't take the time to analyze it. He placed a hand on her waist. "Come on, I'll give you a ride home. Kind of reminds me of old times." He grinned at her.

Shelby moved away from his hand. She saw a flicker of hurt in his beautiful eyes. "I guess I don't really have a choice. Where's your car?"

"I'm driving a truck now." He led her to a blue late-model mid-size vehicle. He helped her in and closed the door before going to the driver's side.

"What happened to your car?" she asked as Taylor pulled out into the road and headed towards her house.

"I decided to give it away."

"Away? Why?" She couldn't imagine someone willingly giving away a car that nice.

"I thought she might enjoy driving it more than I did."

Pain filled her. He'd given his car to a woman. If she'd harbored any hope that he'd come to see her or that there might be a chance for them, she didn't any more. He'd found someone else. She wouldn't let him see her cry. "That's one lucky woman," she said quietly.

"She's very special. There's no one else in the world like her." Shelby didn't have to look at him to tell that he cared a great deal about the woman.

"I'm glad for you."

"Are you really?" He glanced at her and Shelby turned away, preventing him from seeing the tears threatening to spill over. It sure hadn't taken him long to find someone else.

"Yes, I am. I want you to be happy."

"I hope she'll accept it and me along with it."

The fingers of Shelby's right hand clutched the doorhandle as the one in her lap curled into a fist. Why didn't he drive faster? All she wanted to do was get home, close the door and crawl into bed. "Why wouldn't she? You're a great guy."

"I haven't always been. I hurt her and I'm not sure she'll have me now."

"Just tell her how you feel. I'm sure she'll forgive you." Her voice started to break. She didn't want to have this conversation. Giving advice to the lovelorn, especially where it concerned Taylor, wasn't something she was emotionally strong enough to handle.

"So all I have to do is say I love you?" he asked.

She turned to face him. "Why are you here, Taylor? Why're you telling me all this?" Thank goodness he'd turned into her street. She waited for his answer. "Why, Taylor?"

"Because I thought we were friends."

He had a twisted idea of what her friendship meant. She couldn't do this any more. "There's no need to turn into the drive. Just pull up in front of the house."

"I don't think so. A gentleman sees that a lady gets home safely."

She wanted to slap the grin off his face. Didn't he know this was killing her? How could he be so dense?

"Taylor for heaven's sake!"

"Okay, if that's what you want." He pulled to a stop at the end of her drive.

She gathered her camera bag and climbed out of the truck, not looking at him or even where she was going. She just needed to get away. To breathe again. All those hopes and dreams of going to him in Nashville had turned to ash.

Not looking back, Shelby hurried up the drive. She was halfway to the back door when she made out the color red through watery eyes. Rubbing the dampness away, she saw Taylor's car sitting there with a large silver bow on top. She slowly lowered her camera bag to the ground. Her body flushed. "What?"

"As large an apology as I owe you, I figured flowers might not cover it," Taylor said from right behind her. "I hoped the car might ease the way."

Shelby's heart had gone into warp drive and didn't seem to be slowing down. "I kind of like flowers," she mumbled, a grin forming on her face.

"That figures. My little she-cat never disappoints. I come to you with my heart in my hand and you're not satisfied." He chuckled dryly. "Shelby, aren't you going to look at me?" Taylor asked quietly.

"You said you loved the woman you gave the car to."

"I did, and I do. With all my being." He still hadn't touched her, as if he was afraid of her reaction. "I'll live in Benton if that's what it takes. I want you to be a part of my life, every day, always."

She still couldn't move. It was her dream coming true.

"Shelby, please turn around. You're scaring me."

She slowly rotated, looking at him. His dear face for the first time she could remember lacked confidence. Did he really believe she might turn him down?

"Taylor Stiles..." she punched him playfully in the shoulder "...why did you make me think you were talking about another woman?" She gave him a light swat on the shoulder this time before her arms slid up to circle his neck and pull his mouth down to hers. "I love you too," she said softly against his lips. Seconds later he crushed her to him and took control of the kiss.

Some time later Taylor pulled back but didn't let go of her. For that she was glad, she couldn't have stood on her own anyway.

"Nice to see you back, Taylor," Mr. Marshall called. "Planning to stay around, I hope."

"That I am," Taylor replied with such conviction she knew he meant it. "For ever," he whispered into her ear.

"Glad to hear it," the man responded.

Releasing her enough to pick up the camera bag, Taylor said, "Let's take this inside."

It could have been hours or days later for all Shelby knew she was so caught up in the fog of bliss that Taylor created by being in her bed. As she was lounging against him while they ate peanut butter and jelly sandwiches and drank iced tea, she couldn't remember being happier.

"You know, when the man from the service came to get your car, I was sure I'd never see you again."

"I thought it best at the time."

"Why?"

"Because I didn't want to hurt you any more than I already had. Now I know it was because I was afraid. I couldn't say no to you if you asked me to stay again."

"Was I that hard to resist?"

He kissed her shoulder. "Oh, yes, you were."

Then he nipped at the same spot. "Still are. I've been running away. Now I'm running to what I want—you."

She smiled at him. "Uncle Gene said you needed to slow down some, take a look at yourself. I guess he knew what he was talking about."

"You should've seen the look on his face when I told him I planned to marry his niece." Taylor chuckled. A sound she loved.

"When he sent me here I'm not sure he meant for me to join the family."

"What made you change your mind about living here? You were so adamant."

"I found out when I got back to Nashville that I wasn't happy without you and by some measure without Benton. It was a physical hurt to be away from you. I wasn't satisfied with my work, my home or my life there any more. Here I felt good about myself." He paused a second. "I've never seen a healthy relationship up close. Heavens knows, my parents didn't have one. I'm not sure I know how one works. Please be patient with me."

She gave him a gentle reassuring kissed. "Not a problem."

Looking down at her softly he said, "I love you."

"And I love you."

Taylor shifted slightly. "I went back to my hometown. Saw one of my brothers."

She turned and placed a hand on his cheek. "I know that had to be hard for you. I'm sorry I wasn't there for you."

"That's okay. It was something I had to do on my own. I'd like to take you with me to meet my brother some time soon."

"I'd enjoy that."

Buster made a whimpering noise from the floor and Taylor reached down, picked him up and placed him on the bed. "Have you been taking good care of my lady for me, boy?" Taylor asked, scratching Buster behind his ears.

"Yeah, we took care of each other. He missed you almost as much as I did," Shelby said, petting the dog.

"I'm surprised you had time to miss me. I heard all about you being a finalist in the photo contest."

"Thanks to your encouragement and handsome face. How did you know?"

"Mrs. Ferguson," they said in unison.

"You were right about me hiding out here. The

photo contest was my first step towards my new life. I was coming to see you on Wednesday."

"You were?"

"Yes. You just beat me to it by coming here today." She grinned up at him.

"Can I have my car back, then?"

She gave him a playful swat on the belly. "You cannot!"

His mirth was a low rumble in his throat. "What was that you said about my handsome face?"

"I sent in the pictures I took of you at the old house. The judges loved them."

He moaned.

"That's the price you pay for being so good looking."

"You're not hard on the eyes either." His hand slipped under the sheet to run along the ridge of her hip.

She grabbed his wrist, stopping it short of moving up the inside of her thigh. "Before you distract me, let me tell you my other news. I have a doctor who's going to help out at the clinic two days a week."

"So you liked Mark. I thought you would."

Shelby glared at him.

Looking unconcerned, Taylor's gaze focused on her bare breasts.

Pulling the sheet up to cover herself, she said, "You know Dr. Singer?"

He nodded and tugged on the sheet. It slipped to reveal the top curve of one breast.

"You sent him?"

"I did, but his agreeing to work at the clinic was all about your considerable charm. Do you think there's a place for me also?"

"You know there is."

He tugged on the sheet again but she held it securely. "I'd like to lease one of the larger spaces so that we could dedicate part of the clinic to trauma care. The people of Benton and the surrounding area need to have a place close to come in case of an emergency. What do you think?"

"That's a great idea. Thank you, Taylor. You do know that because of you Benton will get to keep its clinic."

His eyes darkened. "I think you should show your appreciation." He gave the sheet a harder tug but she didn't let go, giving him a teasing, come-hither smile. Her heart beat fast when his heated gaze met hers. With one swift movement of his hand the sheet was jerked away and he reached for her.

His lips met hers, replacing the past with the passion of the present and dreams of the future.

* * * * *

Mills & Boon® Large Print
Medical

August

THE BROODING DOC'S REDEMPTION — Kate Hardy
AN INESCAPABLE TEMPTATION — Scarlet Wilson
REVEALING THE REAL DR ROBINSON — Dianne Drake
THE REBEL AND MISS JONES — Annie Claydon
THE SON THAT CHANGED HIS LIFE — Jennifer Taylor
SWALLOWBROOK'S WEDDING OF THE YEAR — Abigail Gordon

September

NYC ANGELS: REDEEMING THE PLAYBOY — Carol Marinelli
NYC ANGELS: HEIRESS'S BABY SCANDAL — Janice Lynn
ST PIRAN'S: THE WEDDING! — Alison Roberts
SYDNEY HARBOUR HOSPITAL: EVIE'S BOMBSHELL — Amy Andrews
THE PRINCE WHO CHARMED HER — Fiona McArthur
HIS HIDDEN AMERICAN BEAUTY — Connie Cox

October

NYC ANGELS: UNMASKING DR SERIOUS — Laura Iding
NYC ANGELS: THE WALLFLOWER'S SECRET — Susan Carlisle
CINDERELLA OF HARLEY STREET — Anne Fraser
YOU, ME AND A FAMILY — Sue MacKay
THEIR MOST FORBIDDEN FLING — Melanie Milburne
THE LAST DOCTOR SHE SHOULD EVER DATE — Louisa George

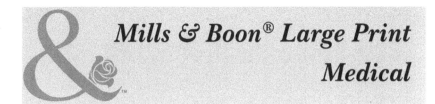

November

NYC ANGELS: FLIRTING WITH DANGER	Tina Beckett
NYC ANGELS: TEMPTING NURSE SCARLET	Wendy S. Marcus
ONE LIFE CHANGING MOMENT	Lucy Clark
P.S. YOU'RE A DADDY!	Dianne Drake
RETURN OF THE REBEL DOCTOR	Joanna Neil
ONE BABY STEP AT A TIME	Meredith Webber

December

NYC ANGELS: MAKING THE SURGEON SMILE	Lynne Marshall
NYC ANGELS: AN EXPLOSIVE REUNION	Alison Roberts
THE SECRET IN HIS HEART	Caroline Anderson
THE ER'S NEWEST DAD	Janice Lynn
ONE NIGHT SHE WOULD NEVER FORGET	Amy Andrews
WHEN THE CAMERAS STOP ROLLING...	Connie Cox

January

DR DARK AND FAR-TOO DELICIOUS	Carol Marinelli
SECRETS OF A CAREER GIRL	Carol Marinelli
THE GIFT OF A CHILD	Sue MacKay
HOW TO RESIST A HEARTBREAKER	Louisa George
A DATE WITH THE ICE PRINCESS	Kate Hardy
THE REBEL WHO LOVED HER	Jennifer Taylor